Appetizers and Alibis:
Alphabet Soup Mysteries

Book 1

Erica J Whelton

Publisher: Sunseri Design Publishing
Cover Designer: Mariah Sinclair Book Cover Design
ISBN: 978-1-956069-25-9

Printed in the United States of America

To my first best friends, my brothers, Ben and Jeff.
You both inspire me to dream big.
Now write those stories!

Books in this series:

Appetizers and Alibis (Book 1)
Biscuits and Bodies (Book 2)
Cornbread and Coffins (Book 3)
Dumplings and Disaster (Book 4)

Other books by this author:

<u>Paranormal Cozy Mystery</u>
Premedicated Murder: Medium with a Heart (book 1)
Replicated Murder: Medium with a Heart (book 2)
Organized Murder: Medium with a Heart (book 3)
Inherited Murder: Medium with a Heart (book 4)
Crafted Murder: Medium with a Heart (book 5)
Destined Murder: Medium with a Heart (book 6)

<u>Small-town Women's Fiction</u>
Mandy's Story: Courage – Finding Herself Series (book 1)
Becca's Story: Purpose – Finding Herself Series (book 2)
Caroline's Story: Serenity – Finding Herself Series (book 3)

The Haunting of Anna-Rose (Paranormal Suspense)
Decoding Us (Women's Fiction/Friendship)

Chapter One

"Incoming," yelled Parker, one of my line chefs, as a ticket began printing. He grabbed it and began calling the order. "Two house salads, shrimp and grits, catfish platter with black-eyed peas and okra."

My team moved in perfect harmony cooking and plating. I watched them for only a moment as I mentally pinched myself at the reality around me. It felt like a dream, but it wasn't. This was real.

Opening day of my first restaurant. Mine. I own it.

I smiled over my shoulder at my sous chef and mentee, Earl, as he plated a dish. He grinned as he caught me watching him.

"Order up!" He shouted.

Like magic, one of the runners, Neal, came for the plates. It wasn't truly magic; it was months of training and determining what the flow of business would be.

As he took those out to the waiting customers, I watched as Eric, one of our bussers, brought dishes to the dishwashers. It was a symphony in motion, and I wanted to giggle.

I'd been working towards this day since I was seventeen years old and won my first cooking competition for my alphabet soup. The recipe was inspired by my Grandmother Ines's chicken noodle soup.

I took that and tweaked it. It got me first prize and started a fire in my belly for competition with my ultimate goal to open my own place.

The place I stood now, listening to the clinks, rattles, and bangs of the kitchen. The stainless-steel gleamed all around me, and heat waves rose above cooking surfaces. This was heaven for me.

"Chef Jess?"

"Yes?" I turned towards Noah, my general manager.

"Lynette from *What's on the Table in Dashwood* would like to speak to you, if you're available."

"I'll be right there."

What's on the Table in Dashwood was a local blog, and Lynette was the make or break it for a restaurant. Stepping to the sink, I washed my hands and face quickly, checked my reflection in the office window.

Earlier today, I had done an interview with *Dining with Nadine*, another local food blogger. It was a fun interview.

"Chef Jessica, so, first question. How did you come up with the name The Crock Pot?" Nadine said, pen at the ready.

"Thanks, good question." I smiled. "What is more comforting than coming home after a long day to something slow cooked with love from a crock pot? It brings up images of mom's kitchen or maybe your grandmother's home. That's what I wanted to create here. Comfort, family, and good memories."

"Oh, I love that. So, I noticed that on your menu you have a soup of the day and then alphabet soup is offered every day. I know only a little about your story, but can you share with me the full story behind your alphabet soup?"

"Yes, when I was in culinary arts high school, my teacher, Mr. Duncan Jones..." I looked over my shoulder at where he was sitting with his wife, Beverly. I waved when they smiled at me. "That's him. He encouraged me to enter a cooking competition with other high schools. The theme was schoolhouse. The ABCs are one of those things you first learn in school, so alphabet soup seemed like the perfect thing. I used inspiration from my grandmother and that was the creation of my recipe. I won and the rest, as they say, is history."

"That's wonderful. Well, I plan to be a regular here."

Now it was time for me to meet with Lynette. She wasn't a soft touch like Nadine. Lynette was old school, while Nadine was my age. We could relate to each other better, and with Lynette, I felt like she was the English teacher you didn't want to disappoint.

Pulling off my scarf that held my hair back, I then smoothed my short dark locks. *A little messy*, I thought, but not bad overall, which is good because I felt like a hot mess. The kitchen had been going strong for the past twelve hours and I had been here the whole day.

I stepped out to the dining area. The place was still packed. I noted that my best friends, Sawyer and Vee, were still at a table near the front window. They caught my eye and clapped silently. They were my biggest fans.

I smiled.

I had asked my family not to come today as I wouldn't have a lot of time to see them personally. My grandmother and aunt had gotten a private tour and dinner a few nights ago when we hosted a family and friends night.

It was a night to do a soft-opening and practice, ensuring we had all the steps and processes in place before opening night. It had been a success.

While my grandmother and aunt had come, my mother and stepfather didn't come. Though that's probably because I hadn't invited them. We didn't get along and I did not need the stress of them.

I continued to scan for Lynette in the two hundred seat dining room. It was amazing to see nearly every seat filled, except for her, sitting alone in a two-seat booth on the left. It made sense that she was sitting alone. Her goal here today was different.

I took a deep breath and made my way to her. I was stopped all along the route by smiling customers.

"Good job, Chef."

"Everything was amazing."

"The alphabet soup was the best thing I have ever eaten in my life!"

"Chef Jess, excellent food!"

I smiled and thanked them all for coming, shaking a few hands along the way.

"Oh, Chef Jessica." Lynette smiled when I arrived at her table. "Would you like to have a seat?"

"Yes, thank you." My body groaned when I sat, but I kept the smile on my face. I'd been on my feet for hours and this was my first time sitting down all day. Minus the two trips to the restroom, that is, but those don't count.

"I just wanted to discuss with you my review before I post it." She smiled, tapping her notepad with her slim fingers. Her perfectly manicured nails continued to drum absently on the pad.

"Oh, I hope it's good." I mentally crossed my fingers.

"Yes, very." She slid her glasses down as she looked at me. "I had the cucumber salad and a cup of the award-winning alphabet soup. As you may remember, I had covered that high school competition all those years ago when I was at the Dashwood Times."

"I remember. Your column boosted my confidence and is one of the many reasons I'm here today."

"Well, aren't you the sweetest," she grinned. "For my entrée, I had the balsamic glazed salmon with scalloped potatoes and green beans. They were superb. How do you do those green beans? I've been making them most of my sixty years, but never like that."

"Chef secret." I slowly grinned at my joke, but it was true. I wouldn't spill how I cooked them. It was a trick Mr. Jones had taught me.

Hearing her laugh at my quip sent a wave of relief through me. I had been so worried that this place would bomb. Though I knew I could cook well, would the public enjoy my restaurant concept? It seemed they did, or at least Lynette did. Her adding credibility and her reputation added another level to my business. I hoped it would increase the traffic coming in.

"Prices are fair, and your servers and staff are friendly. I never once had to ask for a drink refill or a napkin. The decor is classy, yet homey. I love the artwork. Local artists, I assume?" I nodded. She continued. "The environment is upbeat and relaxing. I will definitely be a regular, especially if you have that soup daily."

"That's the plan. It is, after all, how I got here. Well, that and a lot of positive support." I gestured to Lynette.

"I try." She beamed with pride. "Now, I'll take my check and be on my way."

"Oh, Lynette, this is on the house, of course." Something I had done with Nadine as well.

"Well, aren't you the sweetest?"

"Thank you, and I do hope you'll come back to see us again soon."

I walked her to the door, thanking her again, then turned towards my host stand.

"She loved it!" I said to my host and hostess, who were standing there.

"Thank goodness." Jordan squealed.

"We were all on our best behavior," Tyler said with a laugh.

"As I hope we will be for every guest." I looked around, then lowered my voice. "But, of course, Lynette can take us down in a heartbeat if we misstep."

They chuckled, and I went to greet more of the guests on my way back to the kitchen. They all sang praises of the food and service. It was the ego boost I needed.

Pausing at the kitchen door, I turned to watch the flow of my dining room. All the servers were engaging with the guests. The runners were getting food out quickly and people were smiling with each plate. The bussers were cleaning tables fast and getting those tables ready for the next guests.

It all warmed my heart as I turned into the kitchen.

"Earl, we did it. We freaking did it." I high fived him.

"I knew we would." He laughed. "It's a great concept, excellent menu. Plus, it has you."

"And you. I'm so glad to have you here."

"Of course, Chef." He smiled and got back to work.

We had been working side-by-side on this for several months, and in fact, I hired him a year ago when I started planning. Together we built the menu, hired the line cooks, and trained them to make every item to perfection. I couldn't have done it without his support.

An hour later, all the customers were gone, the dishwashers were nearly finished cleaning. We were prepped for the next day.

"Where is Earl?" I asked.

"He took out the trash," Stelly said, thumbing towards the back door.

"But wasn't that ten, fifteen minutes ago?"

"Ah, I … yeah, maybe." She looked at the clock. "He probably grabbed a smoke or maybe took a call."

"Maybe."

He didn't smoke, but perhaps he received a call. I shrugged and finished putting the food away. When I was done, I decided it had been too long.

I dried my hands then pushed the back door open, finding the back parking lot empty of people.

"Earl?"

Nothing. A sound near the dumpster caused me to jump, but it was only a black cat.

"Dang it, cat." I said. I walked around the street to see if he had gone to the front. "Earl?"

No answer.

I ran my hands over my face, then backtracked back to the dumpster. From this angle, I could see it. It was his shoes lying at a weird angle from the side of the dumpster against the wall. I couldn't see him from here, only his shoes.

My blood ran cold as I took a few cautious steps to where he was. I knew what I would find, but I still wasn't prepared for the sight.

I had only seen a dead body one other time in my life. It was the worst night of my life. My father killed a man right in front of me. I never thought I would see another.

As his body came into view, I let out a scream that made even my blood curl. I rushed to him thinking maybe he was just injured. The bullet to the head was probably difficult to survive, and yes, in fact, he was stone cold dead.

Several of my employees came outside and found me holding his body, screaming. I couldn't hear what they were saying, as my mind was buzzing and my body was numb.

Flashing back to the night, my father shot a man. Unlike tonight, it had been raining. I remember watching the blood swirl and mingle with the rain as it puddled all around us. I can't even remember what led up to the fight that caused the shooting.

My father's attorney asked me to be a witness, but I was only five years old and all I could say was my father shot a man. They painted his defense that he was protecting me.

But I could only remember the spinning puddles as the lightning flashed, and the thunder roared above us. I looked up at the man who had always been so tender, loving, and gentle with me, and something in his face had changed that night. It was hard and cold.

I looked at the faces around me now. They were in shock. Some were crying. Most were stoic, watching, wondering, and mumbling among themselves about what could have happened.

He was my sous chef, my right-hand, my friend since he was in high school. We had been working on this concept together for a year. He helped me build the menu, the concept, the entire restaurant. How was I going to continue without him?

Tears fell from my eyes as I held his body.

"I called 9-1-1. They're on their way." Stelly said.

"Who did this?"

"Did you see anyone?"

"We need to check the security cameras."

Murmurs and sobs continued as I heard the sirens in the distance. This was a nightmare.

I let go of Earl and sat back, sobbing into my now bloody hands. Not only was my friend gone, but my business was going to be ruined. It was a selfish thought, but I couldn't help it. This had been my life's work to date, and, in a blink, it was going to be taken away from me.

Just as his life was taken from him.

I felt hopeless and helpless as I continued to stare at the lifeless body.

Chapter Two

I couldn't process what was happening as the officer loaded me into the back of the patrol car. Were they arresting me for Earl's murder? This can't be happening.

I looked out the window of the police cruiser at the confused faces of my staff. Several of them were trying to explain that I was with them all night until just a minute before finding him.

"She couldn't have done it."

"She wouldn't have!"

"She was inside with all of us."

"You can't do this to her!"

They pleaded, but the officers weren't listening.

The scene blurred as I was driven away. My only solace was that it was nearly 1 a.m. and there weren't many curious eyes of the public peering at me and judging.

I cried quietly as we flew through the empty streets towards the police station. It was only a few blocks away, so thankfully it was a short ride.

Once again, my mind took me back to that night when my entire life had been turned upside down at the tender age of five. After the police came to take my father away, my mother was nearly inconsolable. I ended up living with my Granny Ines. She is my father's mother. I love her so much. She was still my best friend to this day.

My mother left me with Granny Ines for two years and only took me back because Granny had to have knee surgery. I would go back to her six months later and spend my time split between both houses until I was twelve when my mother remarried and decided we would be a happy little family.

Too little, too late for me. I wouldn't trust her again.

While that was happening, my father was sentenced to life in prison and had been transferred from the local jail to the prison two hours away. Granny would take me to see him once a month. I hated those visits.

The musty smell of cigarettes, damp concrete, and the sound of crying babies and wives set my nerves on edge. Those sounds and smells were still triggering to me now.

Then there were awkward conversations with my father. He tried to act like everything was normal with questions about how school was or what I planned to do over summer break?

These combined were the reason I wet the bed until I was nearly ten. Sleepovers were a big no-no for years. My grandmother was sympathetic to my plight, but my mother was not. I learned to clean myself and wash my own sheets, so she didn't know about my secret. It kept the peace with her.

Then, after my mother married my stepfather, Samuel, they quickly welcomed my brother Bryan and then, two years later, Christopher. I was already neglected and ignored, but this sent my stock in the family spiraling lower.

Those two rugrats were doted on as if they were the future kings of the world. They could do no wrong and especially when it was at my expense. Being that I was thirteen and fifteen years older, they would get into my stuff and spread it from one end of the house to the other. Then, I would get yelled at for it.

I hated being home, so most nights I would sneak out to meet up with my friends, Sawyer and Vee. We got into so much trouble back then. Petty, silly stuff that wasn't harmful, but wasn't good either.

We would hang out in the park or explore the cemetery. The police would chase us off. Other times, we would egg the house of a bully or a teacher we hated.

But one time, we stole a car. Granted, it was Samuel's car, but he reported it missing to teach me a lesson, or so he says.

"You're lucky it was just your stepfather's car and not someone else's. If you keep heading down this path, you are going to end up in prison. Do you want to end up like your father?" Mom yelled on the way home.

"No." I mumbled. That was my worst fear.

Yet here I was being taken in for questioning in the murder of my friend. It was a nightmare that I really wanted to wake up from.

I blinked my eyes to clear my vision as the tears kept falling. It wasn't a nightmare, and this was the worst day after the best day of my life.

The officer pulled into a spot at the back of the station. He then stepped out, pulling me from the car. I had my hands cuffed, so I was a bit off balance and wobbled a bit.

"Whoa, you good?" He asked.

"Yeah, I guess."

He meant it as a question if I was good to continue inside without falling, but I wanted to yell that no, I was not good as I was being brought in for something I didn't do. I was a victim here, too. Not in the same way that Earl was, but still, someone had shot my employee behind my restaurant on opening day. My memory of opening night was now marred, and the police had the nerve to arrest me.

They checked me in but didn't take a mug shot or do fingerprints or anything like that. It was more of a sign-in thing to keep a record that I was here. That was in keeping with what they were saying about just being interviewed, but, to me, the handcuffs sent a clear message.

"Here. Have a seat. The chief and detective will be in shortly. Can I get you water or coffee?"

"Water?"

"Coming up." The officer stepped out.

I stood there staring at the yellow walls of the tiny room. It held a scratched, dark wood conference table with a few basic conference room chairs pushed around it. There were no windows, no artwork. Just a plain gray analog clock ticking on the wall.

Tick, tick, tick. It seemed to mock me.

I took a seat facing the door. Sighing. I was going to have to call Sawyer or Vee to come get me later. No way would I call mom or Samuel. Even though I was 35 years old, I still felt like a naughty child when around them, and it would be even worse calling from the police station.

I could hear Samuel's scolding tone and my mother's woeful cries. Not worth the heartache.

But the truth was, I hadn't been in trouble in a long time. Not since I was sixteen and given the choice between going to technical school to learn a trade or go to a military style school. I should have gotten over the trauma, but I didn't. It had left an impression on me for sure.

The door opened and in came Chief Cyrus Stone and Detective Richard Upton. The detective had a paper cup that he set in front of me.

"Water," He said.

Chief Stone and I had many run-ins years ago when he was still a patrol officer. He had put on fifty pounds and lost most of his dark hair since then, but overall, he was the same mean-spirited man.

Over the years, I'd avoided him the best I could. This was an unfortunate encounter. I didn't think he handled this type of work any longer, but I guess he saw this as a *special* case.

"Well, well, well, Ms. Vasquez. It's been a while."

"It has." I said. *Thank goodness.*

"So, are *we* going down the same path as your father?" he said flatly, crossing his arms hard over his thick chest.

"No, never. I wouldn't—"

"You were found standing over a dead body." He said flatly.

"That alone doesn't make me guilty."

"Then why don't you tell us what happened?" Detective Upton asked. He had kind eyes and a nice smile. His overall posture and tone were calmer and patient.

Were they doing the good cop-bad cop thing you see in movies?

I decided to focus on him, instead of the Chief. I went through the events of the night from the time the last customer left until I found Earl.

"He was there when we had a staff toast to a successful opening. Then we all started cleaning and prepping for the next day. I saw him taking out a couple of bags of trash, but after roughly ten or fifteen minutes, I realized he hadn't returned, so I went to look for him." I paused as the scene replayed in my head. Finding my friend shot in the head would haunt me for life.

"That's when I found him behind the dumpster." Tears slid down my face.

"Okay, that's good. Thank you." Detective Upton said.

"I'm not buying your story." Chief Stone blustered. "You just *happened* upon him?"

"Why is that so hard to believe? Why would I kill my best employee, my right-hand? Someone I have known for years?" I knew I shouldn't loss my patience here, but I couldn't help it.

"I don't know. You tell us."

This went on for a while, and I was slowly starting to believe that I had killed Earl, which was honestly ridiculous. It didn't make sense and there were witnesses to my alibis. Why was he coming so hard at me?

"I was with my other employees. They all told the officers at the scene."

"You have a family history of this type of thing?" the chief threw out.

"But I have never once shown or done anything violent to anyone."

"You were quite a troublemaker as a teen!" His face red, spit flying from his mouth. He seemed to have it out for me for no reason at all.

"A little harmless stuff twenty plus years ago. I have been a law-abiding citizen since then."

The detective would step in, trying to smooth things over, but the chief would turn on him, accusing him of being on my side. This was spiraling to a place I couldn't explain.

"Stone, I'm on the side of the truth and she has explained. We have witnesses and we have security footage. There is no reason to detain her any longer."

I wanted to hug him. The clock showed it was nearly four a.m., and I only had a few hours to sleep before I needed to be at the restaurant to help open up for the day. It was going to be another twelve-hour day and now, with my sous chef at the county morgue, I would have to step up and do his work plus mine.

"Fine. We'll be in touch." The chief pushed up, storming out of the room.

"I'm sorry about that."

"It's okay. He has a job to do." I tried to give the benefit of the doubt, even though I was seething and wanted to storm out myself.

"Yeah," he looked over his shoulder. "There is pressure from the mayor's office on the whole department, so this is more about mess-ups internally and less about you."

"That doesn't make me feel better." I crossed my arms.

"Well, you are free to go. Do you need a ride home?"

"No, I'll call for a ride." Then I realized I didn't have my cell phone, and I hadn't memorized a phone number in a million years, not since I got a cell phone anyway. "Um, on second thought, can you drop me at the restaurant so I can get my car and stuff?"

"Sure. Let me just grab my keys. Meet you out front."

He held the door of the interview room open and pointed me towards the way out. It was a small station, and I remembered the layout well, but I didn't tell him that.

Standing in the cool morning air, I took a deep breath. *That sucked.*

"Ready?" Detective Upton said, stepping outside.

"Yes." I mumbled.

He pointed me to a gray sedan. As we walked up to it, my eyes fell to the back seat where a car seat, along with a littering of toys and a sippy cup, told me all I needed about him. He was a family guy, and this was not his work vehicle. He smiled.

"I have a two-year-old son."

"Oh." I had no desire for children myself, but that was because of my childhood, not because I hated kids or anything.

He made small talk on the ten-minute drive. I only answered or replied as needed, but honestly, I just wanted a shower and a quick nap before work.

We pulled up, and my eyes darted to the crime scene with the crime tape blowing slightly in the early morning air. There were still two patrol cars there, as a few officers were still taking pictures. They nodded a greeting at the detective.

"Well, thank you for the ride."

I let myself into my restaurant so I could retrieve my car keys, purse, and cell phone. Once the door closed, separating me from the outside world, I collapsed to the floor in tears. The exhaustion, both physically and emotionally, was too much.

What a sucky, sucky night.

Chapter Three

An hour later, I was home, showered, and now lying in my bed. Exhausted, but sleep wouldn't come. It was now a little after five in the morning. My brain would not shut off. I needed to know what had happened to Earl.

He was a charismatic guy, loved by everyone who met him, or so it seemed. Was this just a case of the wrong place, the wrong time for him? Perhaps a petty thief who saw an opportunity and poor Earl was just a nameless victim to him.

That had to be it. I rolled to my stomach, punching the pillow as tears stung my eyes.

I'm glad that I hadn't woken Sawyer or Vee. We all lived together in this townhouse, not far from downtown, and only about six blocks from the restaurant. I could technically walk, but it was just easier some days to drive, especially late at night.

Dashwood was considered a mid-sized town with a population of roughly 60,000 people. However, we were surrounded by larger cities with populations more than double or triple ours. The crime, from those larger cities, didn't always stay where you would expect it to. It seeped into Dashwood from time to time, and there was a robbery, a mugging, or, in the most recent case, my sous chef was killed.

Though I didn't know if that was truly the case yet. I would have to wait for the police investigation to know for sure if it was big city crime creeping in. I really hoped it was that, because thinking someone had it out for him was a harder pill to swallow.

Sawyer had found this place for us a few years ago, but we had lived together since we moved out on our own not long after high school. Nobody we knew was surprised. We had been almost inseparable since we met back in middle school.

Back then, they called us the weirdos and assumed we were in some relationship. But honestly, we were just good friends. I liked to think we were just the misfits of Dashwood. I don't know why I liked that term better. It felt more rebellious, more spiteful.

But the thought of being in a relationship with Sawyer made me laugh, too. He was more like a brother to me.

Actually, Sawyer was a much nicer person to me than my two brothers were. Especially now that they were teenagers. They are selfish, spoiled, and entitled people.

Sawyer is quite the opposite. He was caring, thoughtful, and always knew when I needed a pick me up. He cheered me on at all my competitions, dried my tears when I lost, and was more than willing to be a tester for my new recipes.

I was jolted awake at 9:30 by my alarm sounding. I hadn't even realized I'd fallen asleep.

"It sucks to be the boss." I had no one to call in sick to. I just had to get up and head to work.

There was a knock at my door. I didn't even get to answer before it flew up and both of my best friends came flying in.

"Jessie, oh my gosh, we were so worried." Vee said, climbing into bed next to me, cuddling up to me. She was the most affectionate of the three of us. I had gotten used to it over the years.

"When did you get home?"

"Just before five. Chief Stone still has it in for me. Just like when he was Officer Stone."

"He is the worst. I don't know who thought he should be the chief." Vee made a face.

"Are you charged, or what exactly happened?" Sawyer asked.

The deep frown and worry lines creasing his eyes told me all I needed to know about him. He was an empathetic person and could feel my pain.

"No, I wasn't charged, just grilled for hours. It was awful."

"So, what now?" Vee asked, sitting up.

"I go to work and get prepped for another day, and hope to heck that this doesn't change Lynette's opinion of the restaurant."

"Do you want us to come down there with you?"

"No, no. Don't you both have work? Wait. Why aren't y'all at work?"

"Government holiday." Vee grinned.

They both worked at the post office. Vee didn't need to work because she came from a wealthy family and had a trust fund. Sawyer had no dreams or ambition to do anything but enjoy life. Making the post office the perfect place for him because he loved serving people and actually enjoyed working the counter all day, though he had recently moved to working in the back. He was such a happy-go-lucky guy, and I loved that about him.

Though I was jealous of them today. I needed a day off after this.

"Y'all suck." I laughed.

I ran to the bathroom to get cleaned up and dressed, pulling my scarf around my head. I waved goodbye to my friends who were now on the couch with a movie on. I took one look before shutting the door.

I looked at my car. It was only a few blocks to the restaurant, and my brain was too foggy to operate a car, so I left it there as I made the short walk to work.

I loved this town. It was the perfect small town with a little mix of big town amenities given its proximity to the larger metropolitan area. It had pros and cons, like anything else.

This was an artistic town. Most people here were artists in some form or fashion. Several times a year there were large art festivals where people got to show off their crafts and skills.

I felt that I created art with my food, and I wasn't the only one. We had a large culinary scene here with many great restaurants. That had been one of my worries about ensuring my place stood out.

I rounded the corner to find the front of The Crock Pot was swarming with news reporters. I should have expected this.

Dang it!

I ducked down a back street, then went up one block so I could come in the back way. It would mean going right past the dumpster, but if I could avoid the media for a moment until I could compose myself, that was what I would do.

However, when I opened the door, seeing my employees, I knew I had no time to compose myself at all. I went into boss mode instantly.

"Hey, Chef." Smokes, one of my dishwashers greeted. "You okay?"

"Yeah, how is everyone?" I scanned the kitchen, but only a few people were here.

"A little shook up, but overall, good." Keegan, my day line cook, said coming to greet me.

"Okay, good."

I had thought about closing the restaurant today so everyone could mourn, but a group text said most everyone wanted to move on as normal. Many of them were a lot like me in wanting to get back to normal as soon as possible.

I was of the mindset of keeping busy. If I didn't, my mind would race and cause anxiety. I respected that not everyone was like that, so I would not punish anyone who chose to take a day or two to mourn, even if it meant we were short staffed.

My day shift employees weren't here last night when everything happened. I'm sure many of them didn't find out the news until I sent that text this morning.

I had prepared to answer whatever questions anyone had. That was my job as the boss, owner, and executive chef of the restaurant. But in reality, I was still processing this myself and wish I had someone who could comfort me.

I went into the office and found both Noah, my general manager, and Jenn, the assistant manager. I hadn't expected both of them. The idea had been for them to split their time.

When they saw me, they jumped up.

"Oh, Jess, are you okay?" Jenn threw herself at me.

"Yeah, I'm tired, sad, but overall, I'm okay. You?"

"Poor Earl. I just can't wrap my head around it. He was the best." She said, tears starting down her face.

"How does the staff seem so far?"

"Everyone is pretty shaken up, but hanging in," Noah said.

"They're all throwing their support to you," Jenn said.

I wanted to argue, what else would they do but support me? They all saw me in the kitchen doing cleanup when he was shot. We were all there and had a strong alibi. It had to be someone random.

"So, I guess we need to find a new sous chef?" Noah said, always in business mode.

"Yeah, but not today. I can't even think about it yet. I just want to get through one day at a time." I sighed. "Has anyone talked to the media yet?"

"I said no comment when I came in." Jenn smiled.

"Same."

"Alright. I'll go face the music."

I made the slow trek from the office, through the kitchen, into the dining room. Here I found my front of house staff huddled together. They broke up when I stepped into the room.

"You okay, Chef?" Skye asked.

Overwhelmed, sad, exhausted, frustrated, and perplexed was how I was feeling, but again, I was the boss and had to put on a brave face. Though I had been more candid with my managers, the rest of the staff felt different, so I didn't answer this honestly.

"Yeah, I'm okay. How are y'all doing?"

"Just … worried about the bad publicity this could bring. We had such a successful opening," Ava said.

"And poor Earl," Skye added.

Nods from the others as they agreed with both Ava and Skye.

I could understand her feelings, all their feelings. They were the same thoughts running through my mind.

"I hear you. We just opened, and now, this."

Again, nods from them.

Most everyone got back to work, but I noticed that Eric, one of our bussers, stood nearby. He had been listening, but while everyone else was now preparing for our opening, he was just standing there staring at me. I smiled at him.

"You good, Eric?"

"Like everyone, shocked." He mumbled, then picked up his bucket and walked away.

He was a strange one, but he was polite and quick at clearing tables. Being strange or not had nothing to do with how he did his job. I stared after him for only a second before refocusing on the task at hand.

"Alrighty, wish me luck. I'm going to talk to the media now." I started towards the front door but then turned back to my staff. "Did any of you give a statement yet?"

They all shook their heads.

"Great." I nodded, turned towards the door, and pushed out into the chaos on the sidewalk.

People began shouting questions and swarming into my personal space. It had me backing up against the door. Having that hard surface to lean on made me feel grounded.

"Chef. Chef."

"What happened last night?"

"Who killed Chef Earl?"

"Is it true you were taken in for questioning?"

"Were you charged?"

I stared at the cameras and blurry faces in front of me. It was overwhelming. Nothing in my training or experiences to date had prepared or could have prepared me for this. Who gets training on how to handle a murder at your business? I guess perhaps there were some jobs, but not any places I have worked.

I couldn't say that any longer.

"At this time, I don't have much information. Though it appears to be random."

"Chef Jessica, what about the rumor you were taken in for question?"

"Well, that is true, but not as a suspect. They simply wanted to know what happened." Not a complete lie.

"How do you think this will impact your business?"

"I hope it doesn't. As you all know, we are just getting up and running. We had a successful first day, despite how it ended. We are hoping to have a repeat of that today. One day at a time." I smiled, faking a confidence I didn't actually feel. "Our thoughts go out to the victim's family, and we are cooperating with the police department to help find the person who did this."

They tried to engage me with more questions, but I kept saying that I had no comment, then asked them to leave so we could get ready for business.

"I hope you understand."

Most seemed to be happy enough with the statement I had given, but one lone reporter tried to keep it going.

"I have provided a statement. When we have more information, we will give it." I turned back into the restaurant, locking the door behind me.

I could hear him shouting through the locked door. I groaned.

The dining room was full of my entire staff. I guess the kitchen staff had heard I was going to speak to the media, so they had all come out to join the others.

They stared wide-eyed at me. Now I needed to give them all a similar talk and try to boost morale. I'd have to do this again for the evening shift, I supposed, especially given those were the employees who saw Earl's body.

"Alright, everyone, take a seat." I smiled. "We all know the events of last night were tragic, disturbing, and more importantly we have lost a beloved member of our team. But to honor him, we need to focus and continue with the successful running of The Crock Pot. I know Earl would want it that way."

I paused as murmurs of agreement moved through the staff.

"Now, we will be opening in just twenty minutes. What do we have left to do?"

I asked each section head for an update from the dining room to bartending to the kitchen.

"And the soup of the day is tomato basil." Parker, my day shift line cook, told the servers.

"But I have a feeling the draw will be the amazing alphabet soup," Ava noted. "That was what everyone wanted yesterday."

"Luckily, we have plenty of that one." Parker smiled.

"It's the best soup I have ever had."

"Yes!"

"We see why you won with that recipe."

"Okay, y'all are truly wonderful for saying that." I blushed. This was boosting my spirit and was definitely better then sulking in bed, like I wanted to do. "Y'all are the best staff and friends I could ask for. Now let's get out there and have a wonderful second day."

We broke up, and everyone finished the prep for opening. Soon the tickets were printing, and we were getting food out quickly. The lunch shift went by so quickly.

The fast pace gave me a break from thinking about the murder and loss, though a few times I would turn towards Earl's station to say something, and he wasn't there. It was a crushing reminder.

I took a quick break to eat. I served myself a small bowl of chicken and dumplings. Even though the alphabet soup was a huge customer draw, this was my favorite.

I took it to the bar area to eat in a corner. Ripley came over with a peach lemonade.

"Here you are, Chef. One peach lemonade."

"Thanks." I took a sip. "Wow, I know I've tried this before, but it is so good. Good recipe."

Ripley had brought this recipe with him when I hired him. Maxine, my other bartender, had brought a special iced tea that she taught us. She had an alcohol version and non-alcohol version. I don't know how you improve on either of these drinks, but they did with a few simple ingredients and techniques.

"I'm glad you enjoy it." He smiled with pride and then went back to the other side of the bar.

I scanned the dining room. It was neat and tidy after our lunch rush. Another compliment on the wonderful staff I had. There were a few customers still dining. One was a group of older ladies having a late lunch. Then there was a lone woman in another booth.

We made eye contact for just a brief moment, but an expression flashed across her face. I thought she might rush me from across the room, but that was crazy. I didn't know her.

Ava brought her check so that broke eye contact. I inhaled my food and then went back to the kitchen, taking one look over my shoulder to see if she was still there, but she had gone. I exhaled, getting back to work.

Hours later, we had made it through another day. I messaged Sawyer to see if he would come pick me up, as I didn't think walking home at nearly midnight was a good idea, even though our town was fairly safe. After the events of last night, I didn't want to be caught outside just yet.

I hadn't thought this through. Walking had seemed like a good idea this morning.

He said he would and was on his way.

"Want me to wait with you?" Noah asked.

"Um, no. We live fairly close, so he should be here in a minute or two."

"If you're sure."

I nodded, so he smiled then left me.

I stood near the front door. It was well lit and in a public area, though this was a sleepy little town and by nine p.m. things slowed down, so by this hour, there was nobody out.

I leaned on the door frame, replaying the day in my head. It had been busy, and I was exhausted, but the feedback we were getting from customers made this all worth it. That was my whole goal, to serve good food and make people happy. It was my love language.

A moment later, headlights approached. I pushed off the door frame, but then realized it wasn't Sawyer, so I fell back against the doorframe.

The dark car slowed almost to a stop. My blood went cold as it got nearly even with me, but then more headlights appeared behind it. The car paused only a moment, before squealing its tires as it took off.

My heart pounded as I realized that could have been the killer.

Holy moly. I thought.

Sawyer pulled to the curb. I hopped in.

"What was with that car?" He asked.

"I have no idea. They came up just a second before and stopped. Thankfully, you arrived scaring it off."

"Do you think that's the killer?"

"I don't even want to think about that."

"We should follow them."

He had always been more daring than me, but I was emotionally and physically spent. I needed a shower and sleep.

"I didn't even see which way it went, but honestly, I just want to go home."

He nodded, looked over his shoulder towards where the other car went, but then put his car into drive taking us home.

Chapter Four

Waking up the next morning, before the alarm, I felt refreshed and optimistic, and with my cat on my chest.

"Well, good morning, Lulu."

She meowed. I hadn't gotten to see her at all the previous day, but that's what I liked about cats. Give them food and a clean litter box, and they were pretty much good for a few days.

I rubbed around her ears and under the chin, which were her favorite spots. She started purring and kneading her paws on me.

"Are you looking for some food?"

She jumped up and ran across the room. I knew it. She was not the most affectionate, but neither was I. We worked well together.

I scooped a bit of dried food in her bowl and then gave her fresh water. I rubbed her from head to tail and then went to the bathroom.

A few minutes later, I was leaning against the kitchen counter waiting on the coffee pot.

"Mornin', lovey!" Vee said, coming into the kitchen.

"Good morning, girlie."

She grabbed a mug and got in line. I smiled at her. It was Saturday, so again, neither of my roommates worked, and again, I was jealous. Though I loved my job, I shouldn't complain.

"Feeling better today?" She asked.

"So much."

"How was the vibe yesterday?"

"Tense, stressful. Everyone was sad. But it was still a good day, business-wise."

"That's good." She clapped.

We filled up our mugs. I drank it black, but she went to the fridge for her flavored creamer. Instead of sitting at our kitchen island like we usually did, we sat at our four-person kitchen table.

"So, what're y'all doing today?"

"A little yoga and then hiking."

"I'm jealous."

"We will *definitely* miss you with us."

"Hopefully, I can hire a new sous chef quickly and then I can split days off with them."

"Maybe you should hire two more."

"Not until the restaurant is profitable. I'm already a few employees over what I'm comfortable with."

"But you had planned for that."

"I did, even so, I don't know how long it will take for us to make a profit."

"True."

I had planned for years consulting with a financial planner and a business manager to ensure I understood the ins and outs, and what it would take to open my own restaurant. I had saved most of my winnings from the cooking competitions.

I'd done so many of them because I loved the challenge and meeting other chefs. They taught me new things and pushed me out of my comfort zone. It also honed my skills and focused me on the type of dishes I liked to make.

I also worked in a few different restaurants which further helped me figure out my style and what I was comfortable with. I did elevated southern comfort food with a slight Hispanic influence because that is my family heritage. Mostly, it was my paternal side, and my grandmother was the biggest influence on my style.

She used the entire spice cabinet, fresh herbs, and lots of vegetables. Even when you didn't expect it, there was a pop of flavor or a spice. It was what I had tried to create in my food and why I won that first cooking competition. Lynette even remembers my soup all these years later.

Sawyer came in, his dirty blonde hair going in five different directions and his shorts hanging low on his tall, slim frame. He was a good-looking guy. Someday, a lucky girl would come along and snatch him up, but for now, he was one of my best friends in the world.

"Must have coffee." He mumbled, grabbing a mug, filling it to the brim. "What did I miss?"

"Just talking about work and our day off and nothing." Vee said.

"Are you going to be alone at closing again?" He frowned.

"No, there will be several there with me and tonight, I'll make sure we all leave together."

"Wait? What happened?" Vee looked from me to Sawyer and back.

"You didn't tell her about that car?"

"No. I wanted to forget about it."

"When I got there to pick her up last night, some car took off with a squeal. It looked like it had stopped right in front of her just as I turned the corner."

"It had," I said, replaying the image in my mind.

"Who was it? Did you see?" Vee asked.

"Not a clue. The windows were dark."

"Well, that's not good!"

"I know. I'm glad I got there when I did!"

"Yeah, but I don't understand why someone would be after me, or even Earl, for that matter."

"Hopefully, the police will have some information for you soon," He said, then took a big gulp of coffee.

I looked over at the clock.

"Oh, dang, the morning went quick. I need to get to the restaurant."

"Driving today or want me to take you?" Sawyer asked.

"I'll drive."

"Well, text before you head home. I want to make sure you're good."

I said I would as I rinsed out my mug, then went to my room to get dressed for work. Pulling on my chef pants, t-shirt, and jacket, I then stared at my reflection for a moment. This was a look I had worn for nearly twenty years. Even after all this time, it still brought me just as much joy and pride as it did the first time I put it on.

My life could have taken a much darker turn had Mr. Duncan Jones not accepted me into the culinary arts program. He became my mentor and teacher in one. I was so thankful for him. He had come to eat at my restaurant day one along with his wife of 42 years, Beverly.

"I'm so proud of you, Jessie." He had said when I'd called to invite him.

"I couldn't have done it without you and all the support over the years."

"I just pointed you to the path. You did all the work. You deserve it."

After his lunch, he praised me over and over. It felt so good to have one of my biggest influences there cheering me on.

I grabbed my headscarf and keys, then threw my cell phone into my purse, before heading for the door. As I stepped outside, it began raining. Not just a happy, spring rain, but a full-on monsoon like rain.

Good thing I decided to drive. I thought as I sprinted to my car.

It was a ten-year-old Toyota Camry that I won in a cooking competition. Most of them gave a cash prize, but this one time, they offered a car, and I needed one. Lucky me. It had been a reliable car all these years. I dreaded the day it stopped working, but for now, that shiny blue trophy was my favorite win.

I drove through the wet roads. It was mid-morning, and the street was alive with movement, even in the rain. I love it here.

I hadn't always loved my hometown. It had always been my dream to be a chef in New York, Los Angeles, or Vegas, or maybe even somewhere in Europe. However, after traveling around the country for competitions, spending too many nights to count in hotels and eating too many meals out of a sack, home was where I wanted to be most.

Sawyer and Vee had been by my side through most of it, but with jobs of their own, they couldn't always travel with me. Travel wasn't as fun alone, either. When I was younger, Mr. Jones and my grandmother would travel with me, but once I was in my early twenties, it was all me.

I pulled into the parking lot behind the restaurant. I had gotten lucky on this location. It was on the corner of two busy streets and had a nice front and back lot. Unfortunately, it came at a cost, but it had the potential to make a profit within six months, or sooner, if I watched my expenses and kept the customers flocking in.

But it was still a risk that I wouldn't make it happen. It was a fine line and one misstep, and I would fail.

I stepped inside to find my morning crew was working away.

"Good morning, Chef."

"Hey, Chef Jess."

"Noah is in the office," Parker added.

"Soup of the day?" I asked him.

"Minestrone."

"Perfect. You have it going?"

"You know I do." He lifted the lid on a large cauldron like pot. I peeked in.

"Smells like it needs a little more," I sniffed again. "Basil."

He looked down at the soup and then up at me. "You're the chef."

"Thanks."

I knew Parker aspired to be a sous chef. He was a good, solid line cook and could follow a recipe, but he lacked the vision that was needed, or at least, what I needed, from my right-hand chef. I needed them to be able to create and fill in for me so I could take time off.

Still, I was training him. My plan was to get him to the level he needed to be, so that I could have that second sous chef. For now, I wanted to find someone to be my back up here, and that person would have passion, vision, and the ability to smell the soup to know it needed a little more basil.

I walked through the kitchen, checking the other pots, inspecting the steam tables and prep tables as I made my way to the office. I knew Noah would want to talk about the sous chef's position, and it needed to be talked about. I just dreaded the search.

Earl had been almost a no-brainer when he applied. We had interviewed a lot of people, but Noah had agreed Earl was the best candidate. Not just because of my personal connection to him, but because he had skills and ambition.

"Hey, good morning, Noah." I said, as I finally made it to the kitchen.

"Where have you been?"

"Um, what do you mean?"

"I messaged you earlier and wanted to meet with you before work."

I pulled out my phone. "Nothing," I said, flashing him the screen.

"Well, damn, who the heck did I send that to?" He pulled out his phone. "Oh, whoops, that was a *really bad* date I had gone on a few weeks ago. She'll be confused, but oh well, no matter."

I tried not to laugh at him. He was a good guy, but really one-track-minded.

"I want to get started on the position. We need to have someone else in here and trained because you are going to burn out if you are here every day, all day."

"What about you?"

"I have Jenn. Note she is not here. We worked it out so we can split the days in half. I work days, she works evenings, or at least most days."

"I can take off."

Of course, then I thought about Parker and the minestrone soup. It was a simple thing, but I wanted to ensure that we offered a consistent product. Yes, there could be some slight variation, but overall, the food needed to be a reflection of me. Call it ego, but I just call it my reputation.

"And who will ensure quality control? Who will ensure the kitchen is running efficiently?" He asked.

"Okay, okay. I get it. Earl was really the best at all of that, along with me."

"Yeah, so we need to reach out to the previous applicants and then if those fail, I want to get an ad placed quickly. Time is not on our side with this."

Again, he was good at his job but got hyper focused and a little annoying when there was a task to do. That's why I hired him though.

"I trust you. Give them a call and start doing interviews on Monday starting at nine a.m... I can't do anything after ten-thirty, but then we could probably do more after two and before four. Good?"

"Good." He turned to his desk and started writing notes.

With that little administrative task done, I headed back to the kitchen. No media to deal with today, nothing that would distract me from just cooking and being in the kitchen. It was my happy place.

Ava burst into the kitchen. "Lynette's review is out!"

"Oh, let me see."

She thrust her phone at me. I skimmed the article.

"Oh, my gosh, she loved it!" Thankfully no mention of the murder in her review, at least. "Are there anymore out? Or any news?"

"Are you asking if they are talking about Earl online? The answer is yes, but the Yelp and Google reviews are all fours and fives so far. Positive, positive, positive." As she pointed to various screens on her phone.

"Okay, well good." I didn't want to vocalize what I was thinking. This could kill the business if people blamed me or feared coming, but for now, it sounded all positive and nobody had mentioned the shooting.

"It doesn't look like this is going to hurt us, so don't worry." She laid a hand on my arm.

I smiled. "Thanks."

She turned to the front to prepare for opening in thirty minutes.

I returned to preparing my station and ensuring everyone was ready for the day. Once that was done, I did my usual rounds first to check in with all the employees, making sure nobody had questions, and everyone knew the plan for the day.

"Parker, do the servers all know the soup of the day?"

"Yes, Chef, and it's on the board." He pointed at the whiteboard behind us, leading to the dining room.

I turned to look. "Perfect."

Our bussers for today were Eric and Billy. They were filling their spray bottles with cleaner, ensuring they had clean towels, and everything was ready for the day.

I could hear them discussing music. I didn't know any of the bands they were talking about, so with nothing to add and them looking as if they had everything under control, I moved on to check with others.

By the end of the day, I was exhausted and could see Noah's point about needing someone sooner rather than later.

Chapter Five

Days later, and the news of Earl's murder plus all the positive reviews had only brought in more business. Everyone who came through the door wanted to hear about Earl and also to eat bowls of alphabet soup.

It was a bit of a hit to the ego to think we weren't busy because of our food and service, but because my friend died. Though, with the growing number of reviews online, I tried to tell myself it was also the food.

A small memorial had started to grow around the dumpster. It made it difficult for us to take out the trash or for the trash truck to empty it. However, it felt disrespectful to remove it.

Noah got the ball rolling quickly on the open position and we had already met with a few candidates. Most of our previous candidates already had positions or had moved for jobs, though we had two that nearly quit to come interview. We assured them they did not need to do that.

We hadn't had any luck in the past two days of interviewing. Nobody seemed qualified enough. But I had hope, and we had two more candidates to interview today.

From what many of the candidates said, my restaurant was the one everyone wanted to work at. But if that was the case, why were we having such a difficult time finding someone?

Within minutes, one of the returning applicants reminded me why we hadn't hired her initially.

She was a train wreck. Her hair was dirty, she looked strung out and couldn't follow the simple directions I gave her. When I'd asked her to prepare a dish for us, she didn't have an idea or a signature dish. Having a signature dish wasn't something that I'd required of all my employees, but sous chef felt like a role that would have input into what gets served.

The only positive note was that she brought a set of knives, as I had asked, but they looked brand new, never used. One of them was still wrapped in plastic.

"Well, then, can you show me how you would prep veggies for soup?" We make a lot of soup and dicing and slicing those was a huge part of our prepping.

"Um, okay."

She fumbled around the kitchen, gathering items. She studied each knife before selecting a boning knife and began cutting onions and carrots. Noah and I exchanged a confused look. I had to assume she thought because it was sharp, it would work. However, a chef's knife, like a Santoku would have been a better choice. It is what a lot of chefs that I know use.

I watched her slowly dice the onions into random sized pieces, then she didn't peel the carrots before slicing those. None of them were even close to the same size.

A trained chef would know that's a big no-no, or at least all of those that I have worked with, and Mr. Jones had drilled that into us in school to cut the same sizes.

"Okay, done." She said.

I checked the time. It had taken her six and a half minutes to cut up about a cup's worth of vegetables. That was way too slow for a restaurant. She had no sense of urgency that was needed in a kitchen. We had to be quick.

I probably shouldn't have let her get this far in the process, but I was desperate for an employee. I wanted to make sure I gave her a fair shot.

After watching her fumble around, I vowed not to let anyone else get this far. It was a waste of my time and theirs.

"Thank you."

"Anything else?"

"I think we've got enough information. Thank you for coming. Noah will walk you out." I nodded to him.

He gave a tight-lipped smile as he nodded and then turned to show her out.

As I cleaned up the practice station, I had a mean thought.

I wouldn't even hire her to wash our dishes.

I hate to sound judgmental because once upon a time, someone took a chance on a broken kid. I do understand people fall on hard times, but really if she seemed to have a clue about how a kitchen works, I would have taken at least a chance and found her a position.

Needless to say, I was frustrated with the process and wanted it over. Not to mention, with the increased business, there wasn't much downtime for us to conduct the interviews. I liked to see them move around the kitchen and once we were open, it was difficult to make that part happen.

I had set up a practice station in the corner of our kitchen for the afternoon interviews we were doing. It had worked out okay so far.

Today we had two interviews planned.

Noah and I were waiting for our first interview. The restaurant was quiet with no employees in it. It was almost creepy, especially after the murder and the encounter with the car, though nothing had come from that and nothing else has happened, yet.

Still, I was glad that Noah was here.

"What did you think of the gal yesterday afternoon?"

"Yvette? She was okay. I wasn't sure if she could be a self-starter."

This was another person who we had interviewed. Her demonstration showed she had some skills, but I didn't think she could take on a leadership role.

"That was my exact note on her." He flashed me his notepad.

"If we had a line cook position open, she might work out well."

He nodded.

The front door opened and in came a short, older lady. Perhaps in her mid-sixties. She had purple spiky hair and a beautiful smile. She was dressed in a simple brown skirt with a beige and pink sweater set. It was stylish and classy, but the hair added an edge. I instantly liked her.

"Hi, I'm June. I'm here for the sous chef position." Her voice strong and firm, yet friendly. She set down a well-worn nylon knife storage case.

"Hi, I'm Jessica and this is Noah."

"Nice to meet you both." She shook our hands, and then I gestured for her to sit.

"Would you like a drink? Water, coffee, tea?"

"Water would be nice. Thank you."

Noah stood and went to the bar for a glass of water.

"So, June, we reviewed your resume. Very impressive. But it looks like you haven't worked in a kitchen in about ten years. What have you been doing?"

"Oh, well, I was retired. My husband and I started traveling, but then he passed away. Cancer. I went to live with my daughter for about a year or, oh gosh, more like two, but I started to get bored. I miss the fast pace, friendships, and creativity that only cooking brings."

"That's understandable, and I'm sorry about your husband."

"Thank you, Chef. It was almost three years ago. I miss him, but I know he wouldn't want me to be sad."

Noah came back with a tall glass of water.

"What did I miss?"

"Thank you, dear." She said, sipping at the water. "I was telling Chef about why I haven't worked in ten years and why I am coming back to the workforce at 66 years young."

"Oh?"

She retold Noah the story, and we asked her a few follow-up questions. With every word, I wanted her to keep talking. She had this compelling way of talking and sharing.

"One thing I have asked most of my staff, those that work directly with the food that is, do you have a special recipe or item that you could add to our menu?" I passed her the menu.

She didn't even look at it. "My pimento cheese spread served with crusty toasted slices of bread."

"Really?"

Noah and I both sat forward. Intrigued by her proposal.

"Oh, yes, it could be served as an appetizer in a small bowl." She held her hand out, gesturing a small cup with her hand. "It could be a signature dish of The Crock Pot along with your award-winning alphabet soup."

"You did your homework." Noah whistled. "I'm impressed."

"Of course. I was actually here on opening day. I had lunch with my ladies' grief group. I had the peach caprese salad with a cup of alphabet soup. It was superb." She did the chef's kiss.

"Well, I do like the sound of pimento cheese. Would you be able to make it for us?"

"It takes some time, but I could, yes. Ideally, I need softened cream cheese and then the whole thing should chill overnight."

"Well, we actually have cream cheese softened for our cheesecakes. We can spare some. What else do you need?" I asked.

She listed each item, and what luck; we had everything she needed.

"Let's head back and make some pimento cheese spread," I said.

We stood, and I gave her a brief tour as we made our way to the kitchen.

"Okay, so here is the kitchen," I said with pride.

The stainless-steel surfaces shone and sparkled. It was my dream kitchen come to life. She smiled as she looked around.

"This is beautiful, Chef. You should be so proud."

"Thank you." I walked to the pastry line. "Here is the cream cheese. Then this station over here," I walked across the kitchen, "would be yours."

"Oh, this is nice. Good distance from the fridge, the sink." She looked around and familiarized herself with where things were on the prep table and looked around at the rest of the space. "Okay, I'm ready to start."

Noah and I grabbed stools, sitting back to watch her. She moved around with ease, gathering cheeses, mayo, and other tidbits from around the kitchen. She got the broiler heating; I assumed, for the bread. Then she began grating and mixing, tasting and then adding a dash of this and pinch of that.

She then got a small loaf of bread, sliced it expertly, drizzled a bit of olive oil before sliding it under the broiler. She looked at us with a smile as she cleaned the station.

"We just have to wait for the bread but bear in mind that the cheese will taste better after it chills for at least a few hours but overnight is ideal."

"Of course," I said.

A few moments later, she gathered a plate and then took out the bread, sliding it onto the plate. She spooned a bit of cheese on three slices, then pushed the plate towards Noah and me. She took one as well.

"This looks so good," Noah said, picking up a slice.

We bit into the cheesy goodness. The bread was perfectly toasted; the cheese was creamy with a slight hint of spice from the hot sauce she'd added without being too hot.

"This is amazing." I moaned.

"It is," Noah said, taking another bite.

"Thank you." She spooned more cheese on the rest of the bread and put it on the plate, sliding back over to us.

We finished the treat and then walked her to the door.

"We really appreciate you interviewing with us today and for sharing your recipe," I said.

"We will be in touch," Noah added.

"Thank you both for your time." She shook our hands and then left.

When the door closed and her shadow moved away from the doors, we turned to each other.

"I like her." We said in unison, then laughed.

"I'd say we found our newest employee," Noah said.

"I agree. She is perfect."

"I'll call her later and make the offer."

"Well, we still have that one interview this afternoon, so let's hold off on the offer until after, but I do agree. We likely have our next employee."

He nodded, then strode to the back.

I watched him go as I just stood there processing the interview. June was like a breath of fresh air, vibrant, talented, and she had a natural leadership quality about her. I mostly got all that from watching her work in the kitchen. I have a feeling the rest of the staff would love her as much as Noah and I do.

With that bit of business done, I headed back to the kitchen to see if I could snag another bite of her cheese spread, and then I started my prep for the day.

Hours later, the lunch rush was over, and it was nearly time for our next sous chef interview. We had not yet scheduled other ones, but we didn't think we'd need anymore. Unless this next one blew our socks off, I think we were going to hire June.

Noah came to my station in the kitchen.

"Ready?"

"Is he here?"

"Not yet, but I figured we would get set up."

"Alright, let me just wash my hands and grab a drink."

"Sure. I'll grab us a table."

"Parker, you've got this for a bit?"

"Yes, Chef."

"Thanks."

I washed my hands and face in the sink, then made a stop at the bar for a peach lemonade. I was hooked on those.

"Thanks, Ripley!"

I took a long sip as I scanned the dining room. It was mostly empty, though there were a few customers still eating. I smiled at them as I took my seat next to Noah.

"Did you have time to review his resume?" he asked, passing it to me.

"Oh, thanks. I had glanced at it but didn't read it." I skimmed it quickly. Nothing really stood out to me about this one. "Wait? Did he apply here before? I feel like we didn't interview him last time."

"Really?" He looked down at it. "Oh, wait, I do remember this one now."

"Well, too late now to back out. Maybe he is better in person than on paper."

"Yeah, sorry about this. We just didn't have as many applications this time."

"We didn't have time to wait for more. And after a week of working every single day from 9 a to 11 p, I'm ready for a break."

"Understandable."

At that moment, a man walked in. He was average height and build, dark hair and just plain clothing. He wasn't carrying a knife set of any kind, so perhaps this wasn't our guy. That was until I saw him turn towards us.

We smiled as we stood up to greet him.

"Reggie?" Noah asked.

"Yes, and you are Noah and Chef Jessica?" He asked.

"Yes." We said together.

"Great. Thank you for the opportunity."

We gestured for him to sit.

"Thank you for coming out. Can we get you a drink? Water, coffee, tea?"

"No, thank you." He shifted in his chair. "I'm sorry I couldn't bring any knives. I, unfortunately, don't own my own yet."

"That's okay. We have some you can use."

I was trying not to have negative thoughts, but most chefs at the level we were asking for would have those. Again, benefit of doubt and thinking he could have fallen on hard times.

"Thank you. I'm sure you saw from my resume, I haven't had a lot of experience yet, but I'm trying to get going."

"So, what makes you think you are right for a sous chef position? I mean, you understand what the responsibilities of the job are, right?" There goes the benefit of the doubt from my mind.

"Yes, I understand it is essentially a back up to the executive chef, and yeah, I know I don't have a lot of experience, but what I have is good soft skills. I'm a self-starter. I can follow directions but can also give them. I'm good with people."

"Okay, okay." Noah took a note.

"What is your signature dish? Meaning if you were hired, do you have a dish or menu item that we could add to the menu?"

"Oh, wow." He looked around. "I didn't prepare for that. What type of food do you serve here?"

I wanted so badly to look at Noah for his reaction, but even without looking, I could almost hear him vibrating with frustration. This had been his beef with one of our other interviewees as well.

After that one had left, Noah vented about interviewing 101. It was essential to research the company you are hoping to work for. I loved Noah.

"Ah, we serve elevated southern comfort foods."

"Oh, wow, that sounds good. May I see a menu?"

I should have thought about grabbing a menu. I had done it with the other interviews, but none of them had needed to look at it. That's why I skipped it this time.

Noah grunted and strode to the reception desk. He snatched a menu and brought it back. He pasted on a fake smile as he set it in front of Reggie.

"Oh, this *does* look good. Okay, with this type of menu, I would make … oh wait, you have that already. Then maybe … oh, balsamic salmon right here. Then maybe a side dish." He continued scanning.

I could hear Noah's breathing. He was about to explode.

"Um, Reggie, I don't think this is going to work. We appreciate you coming out, but I think we have all we need to make a decision," I said.

This was the part of being a boss that I hated, the tough love and hard decision part.

"Oh, let me guess, I didn't get it." He slapped the menu shut and pushed it away so hard, it slid off the table and onto the floor between Noah and me.

"That's right," I said firmly without taking my eyes off of him.

"Well, screw you!"

He stood up so fast his chair hit the floor with a bang. The entire restaurant went silent. I was thankful there wasn't a full house. Just a few late lunchers.

"This is why you are going to fail! You think you are some big shot chef because you won a few competitions, but you're nothing! Nothing!"

Marco, one of our food runners, stepped forward. He had been in the U. S. Marines and was huge. I am a big girl, myself. My mother always called me "big boned."

Now full-grown, I was six feet tall and a good two hundred and sixty pounds, I was a force. However, next to Marco, I was a mouse.

"Oh, bringing in muscle!" Reggie puffed up. Marco got closer, gesturing to Reggie to leave. "You are going to regret this! Regret it! I'll be back!"

The door shut behind him.

"Well, that was unpleasant." Noah said, gathering his notepad and the menu from the floor. "I'll call June and offer her the job."

He scurried to the back.

Chicken. I thought as I watched him disappear into the kitchen.

I stood there in shock. Marco came over, picking up the chair.

"You good, Chef?"

"Yeah, thanks."

He nodded and got back to work, as did the rest of the restaurant, including me. I wanted to put that awful encounter behind me.

At least we had our new employee, June. She would bring a breath of fresh air to the place and a new energy. I couldn't wait for her to start.

Chapter Six

June accepted our job offer and would start in a few days. She had a doctor's appointment that she had previously scheduled, and we also wanted to get our paperwork in order.

With that bit of business behind us, we could just focus on making the best food we could.

Today Earl's mother, Vivian, was coming by to clean out his locker here and pick up his last check. It wasn't much, but she should have it. When we talked, she was upset and nervous to come to the place where her son had died.

"But, Jess, I think I'm ready."

"I'm here for you, Ms. Vivian."

"Thank you. I'll see you after lunch."

The lunch rush had been just as slammed as it has been since day one. In fact, it was perhaps busier with each day and with each online review.

Lynette was here today. I hand-delivered her meal to her.

"Here we are, Ms. Lynette. Your alphabet soup with a side of southern pea salad."

"Thank you, Jessie. This looks amazing."

"We appreciate you coming in today."

"My new favorite spot." She smiled. "As long as I make it out alive."

"Oh, um—"

"I was trying to make light of the death. It was actually very sad, dear." She reached her hand, taking mine, giving it a quick squeeze before releasing it. It was a sweet gesture.

"Yes, he was a good friend and chef."

"I didn't know him well, but he did seem like one of the good ones."

I nodded.

"I heard you hired Ms. June Clearwater as your new sous chef."

"Yes, she'll start in a few days."

"Smart move. She's outstanding."

"I'm glad to hear that." I smiled. "Well, enjoy your meal and, of course, it is on the house. Oh, and your favorite bread pudding is our dessert special. I will have them wrap you up one to-go."

"Aren't you just a doll? Thank you, Jessie."

Since Ms. Lynette had known me since I was a wayward teen, she was one of the few that called me Jessie. Most, even some in my family, called me Jess or Chef.

An hour later, I had my station prepped for the evening. Then I washed up and took a sandwich to the bar for my lunch. I sat in the far corner.

I liked to sit here so I could watch the dining room. We had few customers at this time, but it still allowed me to observe the staff that I wouldn't normally get to see from my place in the kitchen.

"Here you are, Chef." Ripley set a lemonade in front of me.

"You know, I probably should cut back on this."

"Want me to take it back?"

"Try it and see how fast you lose a hand." I laughed, taking a big gulp of the tart and sweet drink.

"Ha, alrighty." He backed away with a chuckle.

I ate my turkey sandwich and watched the door. I was hoping to finish before Vivian got here.

My body was heavy as I sat there. I have been working fourteen-hour days for two weeks now. Once June starts and is comfortable, I'm going to take at least a day off, if not two in a row. My plan was to sleep and take a long bath and then sleep some more.

But I hadn't spent much time with Sawyer and Vee lately and I missed them. They were on my list of things to do when I started having regular days off again. We had plans to go for massages and have a movie night. I also needed to pull my weight around the townhouse. They had been cooking and cleaning the place, but to be fair, I wasn't there to mess it up either.

"Need anything, Chef?" Ava came over to check on me.

"I think I'm good."

"Here, I can take your plate."

"You're amazing."

"So, Earl's mom is coming?" She whispered as she gathered my plate and napkin.

"Yeah. I feel like I failed her, even though I know I didn't."

"Well, I know I wasn't here, but how could you have known it would happen, or what could you have done?"

"I know that logically, but still, some guilt."

"Well, don't beat yourself up. K?"

"Thanks, Ava." The front door opened. "Oh, she's here."

I stood and went to greet her. Even though my whole body screamed for me to sit back down, I pushed myself forward. It was best to keep moving.

I saw her scan the restaurant, then touched a tissue to her eyes. I'm sure she was thinking about how this was the place where her son died. Perhaps it wasn't quite so morbid, and maybe a little more like *this is the place my son loved and helped to build*.

"Ms. Vivian, welcome."

She was a beautiful woman. The type that aged well and made you question how she could possibly be her age. With her stylish bob haircut to her perfectly manicured nails to her knock-off designer clothing, which looked like the real thing, she was posh and timeless.

But it was more than her appearance, she carried herself with a confidence that radiated through her. Her energy could brighten the darkest day.

"Hi Jess, thank you for taking the time for me."

"Of course. Do you want to gather his things first or—"

I didn't say the rest of what I was thinking. I hated taking out the trash because each time I did, my mind flashed back to seeing Earl's lifeless body laying right next to the dumpster. Of course, with the memorial and flowers still in place, the trash company moved the container over a bit, so they didn't have to fight to gather it.

Someone from the city or police department came to clean up the blood. I honestly was still in shock, so I didn't pay attention to who did it. However, there was still a slight discoloration of clean concrete where he laid. It was a constant reminder.

"I'd like to see it."

"Okay, let's walk around."

She nodded, and we stepped out the front door. The sun was bright in the sky, and I wish I had brought my sunglasses out. My eyes were so sensitive to the sun and bright lights in general since I worked inside most of the day. But I remember even back as a child, my eyes were sensitive.

Oh well, I can suck it up for a few minutes.

We turned the corner to head to the back parking lot. She started weeping as the flowers, stuffed animals, posters, and various pictures came into sight.

"Here?" She pointed to the slightly brighter area.

I nodded, as the lump in my throat wouldn't let me speak. I could still see his lifeless body, blood pooling around him. The putrid rotting smell from the dumpster mixed with the iron like smell of blood was still fresh in my mind.

My stomach churned, and my heartbeat quickened at the memory. I tried to take deep cleansing breaths.

We stood in silence. She walked around looking at the various items, dabbing at her eyes at a picture of him or a poster with a message of love.

He had been a popular kid in high school. Everyone knew him. He was a few years younger than me, so I graduated before he started in the culinary arts program. Mr. Duncan Jones and I still worked together, so I often spent time at the school. He had taken me on as a teacher's aide. That's when I first met Earl.

"He was a perfect baby," she mumbled. "He wasn't perfect as a teen, but he was lovable and had a good heart."

"He did."

We stood in silence looking at the memorial, each lost in our own thoughts for several moments.

"This doesn't make sense at all," she finally said.

"Have the police given you any information?" I asked.

The pained look in her eyes had me regretting the question immediately. But I hadn't heard anything from them since they took me in for questioning and I wanted to know if she had.

"Nothing. Only that the security footage didn't show much. Apparently, the video doesn't go all the way to here." She pointed to an area just outside of our parking lot. "And he was facing this way arguing with someone who was just off camera."

"But they don't think it was me, right?"

She looked me over from head to toe as if trying to decide if she thought it was me.

"No, they don't. Earl really looked up to you and was thrilled to have gotten this job. He walked on clouds for weeks, bragging to anyone who would listen to him." She half-laughed, half-cried.

"I was so excited to have him." I choked a little. I didn't want to cry, not in front of her when I was trying to be strong for her. "Do you know anyone who had a beef with him?"

"None at all. Though I do know that he was getting threats after he took the job."

"Threats? Really? Why?"

"They said that he didn't deserve this job and if he didn't give it up, he would be sorry." Tears started down her face. She didn't even try to wipe them away. "He wasn't going to tell me, of course, but he took a call once in front of me. I wish I had pushed him to report it to the police. He laughed it off as a prank."

I fought the urge to hug her, because while I knew her casually for years, I didn't know if comfort hugging was part of our relationship.

"Wow, I'm sure you told the police."

"Yeah, well, after … but they thought it was just harmless. Ha, harmless. My son is dead. My only child. Gone." She mumbled something else that I couldn't understand. It might have been a curse on the police department, but I'm not sure.

We stood there for a few minutes, staring at the memorial. I hadn't wanted to spend a lot of time out here, because it just reminded me of that night and the one from my childhood. My guilt weighed heavy on my heart. I started to say something to Vivian when a car came around the corner.

It was a dark sedan, much like the one last week.

Where we were standing was only a few feet from the roadway. Panic filled me as it slowed next to us. The passenger window rolled down, and a gun appeared.

I pushed Vivian out of the way as I also dove for the ground. We hit the ground as the shot rang out.

Tires squealed, and it was gone. Things happened so quickly that I didn't have time to get a good look at the car or the license plate. Nobody was visible, just the hand, and a gun were all I saw.

"Oh, my. Are you okay?" I asked her.

She sat up trying to catch her breath. "Yeah, I think so. Thanks for pushing me."

"I need to call the police." Though I didn't want a run in with Chief Stone.

The back door opened and out came a number of employees. Parker was on the phone. It sounded like he was calling in the shooting already.

"No, it doesn't look like anyone was shot." He looked at us. "Are you both okay?"

"Yes, a little scraped, and a lot scared, but okay." We both had scraped knees, and I had one hand with road rash.

I looked over at the fence behind the dumpster. It was splintered where the bullet hit it.

"Did you see anything?" I asked Vivian.

"No, I was looking this way and had you not pushed me, well, I can't even think about it." She sobbed. I wrapped my arms around her. We cried together.

We waited for the police officers, then gave our statements. They collected their evidence, and we provided them with the security footage. I had a feeling it was going to be much like the other and nothing would be caught.

They were going to check the CCtv at the surrounding businesses and the traffic cameras to see if they could catch a car fitting my vague description.

With that bit of business done and it now being time for our dinner rush, I quickly helped Vivian gather Earl's things and gave her his check.

"Please let me know if you need to talk or want to come in for a meal. You are always welcome here."

"Thank you, Jess." She hugged me.

I watched her leave. I hope she wasn't in danger. It was either her or me that they were after. I shivered at the thought. Then got to my station to get caught up on food orders.

Chapter Seven

Two days later, there were no new developments in the shooting or Earl's case. Detective Upton had stopped by earlier this morning asking more questions.

"Have you had any issues or threats?"

"No. Nothing that I can think of." I said. "Oh, well, we had a guy upset that we didn't hire him, but that was after Earl was shot."

"Um, maybe we should talk to him. You still have his name and contact information, I assume."

"Of course." I started digging through the desk that Noah, Jenn, and I shared.

Our office was an organized mess. One large desk and five chairs. Why five? I don't know, but when we were planning, it was suggested, one for each of us plus two extras in case we had employees join us. We had a large gray file cabinet with all our business files in it and then our safe was kept in here.

On the wall were two large white boards. One we used to figure out the schedule, which was then put in a private online scheduling application for our employees. The other was brainstorming. Nothing fancy.

"Here. Reggie Reardon and we have a cell phone number. No address." I passed him the resume.

"Alright. This will help." He skimmed it quickly.

"Were you able to get any information about the shooting from the traffic cameras or from the other businesses?"

"We have a bit but still gathering information."

I felt like he was holding back slightly, but why? What was he hiding?

"Oh, I thought … you don't have anything?"

He sighed. "Okay, Chief doesn't want me to share too much, but yes, we saw a car. Unfortunately, it has paper tags that are quite faded. We couldn't pull any registration, but we have the entire police department looking for a car with the general description."

"Okay." I knew the chief didn't like me, even after all this time, but why can't he share some information when I was shot at? "Thank you for telling me."

"Well, if you have any new threats or anything suspicious happen, please, please call me. Day or night." He passed me his business card. "My wife and I just had a baby recently, so between her and the two-year-old, we don't sleep."

"Oh, congratulations on the new baby."

"Thanks." He smiled.

"Do you want anything to-go? Peach lemonade or iced tea? Maybe some food?"

"Oh, thanks, maybe a lemonade."

"Good choice."

We walked to the bar, and I got a to-go cup, filled it with ice and then lemonade.

"Here you go," I said, handing it to him with a straw.

"Oh, looks good." He tasted it. "Wow, that's amazing."

"It's all Ripley." I pointed over at him.

"Hats off to you."

"Thanks." He grinned from his spot behind the bar.

"I'll be in touch, Chef."

"Thanks."

I stood there as he walked out. This had not been what I had expected when he showed up. I thought he was going to give me a name, tell me they had made an arrest, and the person would be put away forever. Isn't that how it worked on TV?

But this wasn't television, this was real life, and it was my life.

I stopped my daydreaming to do a lap around the dining room. I didn't get out here too much, but I liked to check in on things from time to time. I said hello to the few diners, asked about their experience, and what they had chosen.

"Oh, the chicken and dumplings are my favorite too."

"You had the catfish? That's a good choice."

"Thank you for coming out."

"We hope to see you again."

Once I greeted them all, I did a check in with my servers and bussers. My servers today were Ava, Skye, and Faye. The two bussers were Eric and Andy.

"We are getting a lot of questions about the shootings. Plural." Ava frowned. "What the heck is going on? Are we safe?"

"The detective said we shouldn't worry, but they are still checking on things."

"Well, I don't know about you, but I think we could do a better job of finding this person or people than they are," Skye added.

"Ha, can you imagine? Me, a private detective. Chef turned investigator."

We laughed and then got back to work, with me returning to the kitchen to get ready for the evening. June would be starting with us, so I wanted to make sure everything was ready for her to come in. I had a feeling she was going to hit the ground running.

She'd requested the evening shifts. The plan was for me to do day and then she would come in to do the evening shifts. That would give me half a day off. It was a hell of a lot better than what I was doing now. I couldn't wait.

I was also training Parker to take over some of my job duties so that he could fill in for me or June when needed. He wasn't quite there yet, but each day he got a little better.

While I was setting up June's station, Ava came back.

"Chef, there is someone here claiming to be Earl's girlfriend. Says she wants to pick up his stuff and his final check." Her confusion was written all over her face. "Didn't his mom pick that up?"

"Um, yeah, but just —" My intuition said this was a scammer. "Tell her I'll be right there. Have her sit at the bar? Stall her as long as you can. I'm going to make a call. Oh, but don't tell her that. Just say I'll be out in a moment."

I went to the office and dialed Vivian's number. She didn't answer, so I just left a "checking on you" voicemail. No point getting her worried about nothing. Next, I called the detective.

"Detective Upton." came his deep voice over the phone.

"Detective, this is Jessica Vasquez over at The Crock Pot."

"Oh, hi, Chef. What's up?"

"I know you just left, but someone showed up claiming to be Earl's girlfriend here to pick up his things. But as you know, his mother did that the day before yesterday. As far as I know, he wasn't dating anyone and even if he was, nobody serious enough to pick up his stuff like this."

"And you think it could be linked to the case?"

"I honestly don't know, but I thought it was worth calling."

"Okay, try to keep her there. I just got home so I could help my wife for a bit, but I will head that way in just a few minutes. Shouldn't be long."

We hung up. I plastered on a smile. "Do I look confident?" I asked Noah.

"Sure. Good luck. You want me to come with you?"

"No, but maybe be nearby. I'm so bad at describing people, we might need that skill."

He nodded and followed me, stopping just before reaching the dining room and bar area. He waited.

I continued on. Ava pointed to the lone woman at the end of the bar. She looked familiar, but I couldn't place her.

"Hi, I'm Jess and you are?"

"Fern, Earl's girlfriend, but I'm sure he talked about me all the time." She flipped her purple and black hair.

"Um, sometimes, yeah." I lied. I mean, if she was going to, I could too.

"I'm just so broken-hearted to have lost him." She worked up a few tears. "We were talking about getting married, starting a family. Now he is gone."

"Yeah, it is a great loss to all of us."

"Yes, truly." She grabbed a bar napkin to wipe at her fake tears.

"You probably know, he didn't keep things here and his check isn't ready yet. We have our admin getting it prepared now."

There was no admin. Noah cut all the checks.

She flew off of the bar stool as if it had been kicked out from under her.

"That is unacceptable! He told me he kept an extra outfit here and some important paperwork. He felt it was safer here than at home. And I need that money. We have rent due. How am I supposed to pay it alone?"

"I understand, but if you just wait for a few minutes, we will have it ready. I can tell you we don't really have lockers here. I mean, we have a few, but not enough for everyone to keep stuff here. It was mostly for use during the shift." A partial lie. Only a few of us kept stuff long term and most of us doubled up.

"That's not true. I've seen the lockers. You have—" Her face went flat. "I need to go."

She darted from the bar and out the door. I looked for Noah; he had come into the area and moved close to the host stand.

He ran out the front door behind her; I hoped to see if he could catch a car. He returned a moment later, shaking his head.

"She was not in a dark sedan. It was a small SUV. Mazda, I think."

"Did you recognize her?"

"Yeah, I think I do, but I can't think of her name. I believe she was one of the sous chef candidates from last year before we hired Earl."

"Really?"

"Yeah. She didn't have a lot of experience but had a good attitude. That is, if I am remembering correctly."

"Was she blond then? I think I might remember her now."

"Yes, I think her hair was blond."

My mind finally caught up, remembering where I saw her last.

"She was here after Earl died. I thought she was going to come at me."

"Really?"

"Yeah, but I didn't think anything of it at the time. We have a few things we've been dealing with." I shrugged.

I didn't want to keep thinking about Earl's death. It was hard not to because we had gotten so close, especially once he started working here. I had known him for years.

That's when Detective Upton walked in.

"Where is she?" He looked around as the two of us just stood there alone.

"She left."

"As if she was on fire." Noah added.

"Really? Did you figure out what she wanted and who she was?"

I filled him in on the conversation and how we knew her.

"Do you have a name?"

"She said Fern." I looked at Noah.

"I can look again at the resumes. I still have them, but I don't remember seeing a Fern."

The three of us went back to the office, but I got pulled into the kitchen. Parker had a question about our recent food delivery.

"We had checked it all in, but I feel like we might be missing something."

"Okay, I'll come check." I looked at Noah and the detective. They nodded.

I went with Parker to review things. After five minutes, I managed to find the missing chicken and pork he couldn't find. This was just an example of what we were still working on with him.

"We're good?"

"Yes, Chef. Sorry." He looked at the ground.

"I don't want you to be sorry. Asking is learning."

"Thanks." He smiled and got back to work.

It was nearly the end of his shift, and I didn't want him to feel bad. He was the type that beat himself up over little things.

Some kitchens were rough places and making a mistake would get you chewed out, but I didn't want that type of environment here. I wanted to create a positive work environment where everyone could grow and feel like they could ask questions, make mistakes, and learn.

I went to catch up with Noah and Detective Upton. They were chatting and sorting through resumes. Between all the positions we had, there were a ton of them. I couldn't even guess. A hundred or more, maybe.

"Here, I can look through a stack." I said. Noah handed me some.

We flipped through them quickly, just looking at the names. As I flipped my last one, I looked up.

"Any luck?"

"Nope. Not in mine."

"No Fern."

"As I thought, it was a fake name." I looked down at the stack. "I can't even think of what her real name is."

"Well, Noah gave me a description. I will head back to the station and see what I can find, if anything. Thank you for calling me though. This is exactly what we need, more clues."

After he left, I thought about what he said and what Skye had suggested. Perhaps I should start looking into this. With June starting, I would have time off, so it was doable.

It was something I was really going to have to think about, especially if it was going to have such a huge impact on my business.

Chapter Eight

As I had expected, June had hit the door running. The staff instantly took to her. When she gave an order, they followed as if she was me.

It was a huge relief because it meant I was going to get some time off, finally. Today was my first day off, and as I walked into the townhouse before my roommates, it was a weird feeling. They weren't asleep or out with friends or even watching a movie without me. Oh no, not today. They were still at work.

I did a little happy dance.

Lulu came to greet me. She meowed at me as if asking why I was home.

"Hey, kitty girl." I scooped her up. "Mom's home early."

She meowed.

"No, I didn't get fired. I'm the boss."

She meowed again.

"I don't care if you believe me, that's the truth."

She pushed away from me, so I put her down, but she started rubbing against me. I bent over to pet her, starting with some chin scratches then down her from head to tail a few times before she moved away from me.

Once she was satisfied, she pulled away from me.

"Okay, you done?"

As she walked away, she looked once over her shoulder at me. I chuckled as she disappeared up the stairs and into Sawyer's room.

I followed behind her but turned into my room and headed for the shower. My normal routine was to wash the kitchen off me before I could relax.

It was nice to take my time in the shower, actually shave my legs, and not yawn through the entire process. I even took the time to condition my hair. It was a luxury I had missed.

I had thick, coarse hair, but I kept it in a scarf or tiny ponytail most of the time. Even when it was down, it wasn't long, going to the top of my shoulders. I didn't like it much longer than that. It just didn't work for my lifestyle or even who I am.

I toweled off, grabbed my softest leggings and an oversized t-shirt. I shook out my hair, leaving it down so it could air dry.

"Better." I sighed.

That's when I heard Sawyer and Vee. I ran down the stairs.

"Surprise!" I jumped at them.

They laughed.

"You're home!"

"You are *REALLY* home." Vee yelled, grabbing me.

"Yes, I did it. Finally!"

"We are so excited to have you here," Sawyer joined our hug.

The three misfits are back together. I thought.

"So, pizza and movie night?" Sawyer asked.

"As long as I don't have to cook, I'm good." I laughed. While I loved cooking, and normally wouldn't mind, one night off felt good.

"No cooking for you tonight, Chef Jessica!" Vee teased.

They went and got changed from work. I settled into my favorite spot on the couch. It was in the left corner. Our sofa was a soft and fluffy microfiber thing that we had had for years. I pulled a blanket around me as I settled in with the remote.

Sawyer was the first to join me. He plodded into the matching oversized chair. That was his spot.

"June is working out then?"

"Oh, my gosh, yes. She's wonderful."

"I'm so glad. We were worried sick about you."

"To be honest, I was getting worried about me, too. I was heading straight for burnout."

This wasn't the plan. I had worked it out perfectly for more than a year with Earl. We were going to switch out our days off. Together, we had carefully designed how the restaurant would work, right down to our schedule. I mean, I had it partially planned for a while, but he had helped me frame it better.

We sat there in silence, watching a cooking show on the television. After I'd won one specific high-profile competition, I was asked if I wanted to host a cooking show or a food reality show. I politely declined. That was not me. Though I did enjoy the competitions.

"That could be you," Vee said, coming into the room, taking her spot on the couch. It was on the right hand side, opposite me.

"Are you reading my mind again?" I chuckled. "I was just thinking about that offer I got."

"You would have been amazing."

"Ha, I just like what I do."

"Okay, did you ask her yet?" Vee asked Sawyer.

"Ask me what?"

"No, I didn't. I was waiting for you."

"Someone ask me." I chuckled.

"We were just curious about what is going on with Earl's murder and then, of course, you getting shot at. Is there any news about that?"

"No, blah." I groaned. "It's awful. I keep waiting for the other shoe to fall on this one. When will it happen again? Or even, if it will happen again? Obviously, I don't want it to."

"What are you going to do?"

I eagerly leaned forward. "Okay, so this is going to sound super crazy, but Skye asked why I, or I guess she actually said we as in us employees, but anyway, why don't I look into things. You know, be like a private investigator or something, like on TV."

"Really?"

"I wanna help!" Sawyer blurted.

Vee looked at us both.

"You are *both* crazy, ya know that, right?" She said.

"But you're going to help, right?" Sawyer asked her.

"Of course I am, but I can still think you are crazy for even considering it."

"Yes, you can."

"When do we start?" he asked, bouncing with excitement.

"Not tonight. Tonight is pizza and a movie and me right here in my spot." I sat back on the couch with a sigh.

My phone rang. The display said Vivian.

"Hello?"

"Jess, it's Vivian."

"Hi, Vivian. How are you?"

"Not good. Not good at all. Are you at the restaurant?"

"No, I'm at home. What's wrong?"

"I received a threatening message, and I wanted to show it to you."

"Me? Why?"

"It's on a receipt from The Crock Pot."

"Oh, wow, okay, yes, come over. I'll text you our address."

"That's okay. I remember where you live. I picked Earl up from there a few times."

"That's right. Okay, see you soon."

She had met Vee and Sawyer before, so it wouldn't be a surprise to her that they were here as well. Movie and pizza would have to wait until she left.

About twenty minutes later, there was a knock at the door. I jumped up to answer it. Opening it I found a distraught-looking Vivian.

"I'm so sorry for this. I guess I should have gone to that detective, but frankly, I'm not getting a positive vibe from the police. And maybe it's nothing or maybe it's something, so before I get them involved, I wanted your thoughts."

"Yes, of course, come in." I gestured towards our kitchen island. "Have a seat. You remember my friends Sawyer and Vee?"

"Yes, of course, hello, dears."

"Hello."

"Can I get you something to drink? Water, tea, coffee?" I offered.

"Oh, tea would be nice. Thank you."

I moved to our electric kettle and filled it up, starting it to boil.

"Here, I'll do it. You talk." Vee offered. "English breakfast good?"

"That's my favorite." Vivian said.

"So, you said you got a message?" I asked as I took a seat on the barstool next to her.

She pulled a paper out of her purse, passing it to me. It was definitely a receipt from my restaurant. The date on it was worn so I couldn't tell which day it was, but I could see that Ava was the server.

It read: ***Give me back what's mine or else***.

"Wow, give back what?"

"I have no idea."

"I should call Detective Upton. Do you mind?" Which is likely what she should have done, but I'm glad to see this. Though I had no idea where to go with it from here. If it had more legible details, I could have come up with a plan.

"Go ahead."

I stepped away to get my phone, then dug his card out of my purse. At this point, I would need to save this into my contact list.

"Hello, this is Detective Upton."

"Hi, Detective. This is Jessica Vasquez."

"Ah, Chef! Is something wrong?"

"Yes, actually. Earl's mother, Vivian, received a threat. It was written on a receipt from my restaurant."

"Any idea who left it?"

"No, but I thought you should see it."

"Are you at the restaurant?"

"No, I'm at home and she is here with me."

"Alright, send me the address and I'll be by soon to check it out."

We hung up, then I texted him my address. Then I turned to my friends.

"He's coming over to have a look."

"Thank you," Vivian said.

"Can you run this number through your point-of-sale system to see what day it was? I mean, since the date is worn off," Vee said as she examined the receipt.

"That's a good idea, but I can't run over there now that he is coming here."

"What if he keeps it?" Vee asked.

Sawyer grabbed it and ran to his room. He came back a few minutes later.

"I scanned it into my computer, then printed a copy. We will have an electronic copy and a hard copy for you to take to the restaurant. Just don't tell the detective. He might not like that."

We agreed, including Vivian.

While we waited, we visited and sipped our tea. We kept the topic away from the restaurant and Earl as much as possible.

There was a knock at the door. This time Sawyer went to answer it. I heard him greet the detective and ask him in. Then the two joined us in our kitchen.

"Hello."

"Hi."

"So, you received a threat?"

"Yes, it was taped to my car window. I found it when I was going to run errands earlier."

"And you came here?"

"Well, I wanted to ask Jess about it since it was on a receipt from her restaurant."

"Any ideas?" He looked at me.

"No, but I was thinking I could look in our point-of-sale system to see if I can narrow down the date and time. Then we could check security footage of the front door to see if we can get an idea of a suspect."

"Good idea. Is now a good time to check that or should I come by in the morning?"

I looked at Vivian. I knew she was worried and would continue to be stressed about it until we figured it out.

"We can go now. It shouldn't take too long to find in the system, but the security footage could take a bit."

Sawyer and Vee stayed behind. Vivian offered to drive me, and then the detective followed us.

"Now with two car seats in my personal car, it is a bit crowded in there," He said.

I think he meant it as a joke, but we didn't laugh.

Vivian and I drove over in almost silence, just the quiet radio playing smooth jazz. I actually loved this stuff, even though most people my age wouldn't listen to it. I found it relaxing, and it reminded me of my Aunt Rita. She loved to listen to this as she slowly danced around the living room with a bottle of wine.

She'd never married and always lived with Granny Ines. They said they were best friends, even if they were mother and daughter.

We pulled into the restaurant.

"Do you mind if we go around back? I really don't want to bring more attention by us traipsing through the dining room. I have enough attention with the huge memorial." Immediately, I wanted to kick myself. "Sorry, that's insensitive, but you know what I mean, right?"

"Yes, dear, I get it." She lightly touched my arm.

We got to the back door, I punched in the code and let us inside. All eyes turned to us.

"Sorry, y'all. Just need to check something in the office." I smiled. "How's it going, June?"

"Excellent. I love this kitchen." She grinned and kept plating the salmon in front of her.

We got to the office to find Jenn here. I knew that, but she was shocked to see me.

"I thought you were taking today off."

"Yeah, but we have a little bit of police business."

"Is this about Earl?" She gasped and looked at Vivian and the detective.

"Yes. I need to check this receipt in our system."

"Here, let me see." She typed up the receipt number, and the result was instant. "This is from day two at around 1:30 in the afternoon."

"Oh, great. Can we pull up the security footage for around that time?"

She pulled up our security software and then searched for the day and time, then hit play. We all gathered around her to watch the footage. Most times the ticket was cashed out, the person left within about ten minutes or less. We played the video for several minutes.

"Did you see anyone you know?" Detective Upton asked Vivian.

"No, nobody. Well, a lady from my Bible study, but I know it wasn't her. Her handwriting is very elegant, and I would recognize it. She always sends handwritten greeting cards for birthdays and holidays."

"Darn. Do you think someone just found a scrap of paper? Like maybe in our trash?" I asked the detective.

"Anything is possible." He looked at Jenn. "Can we get a copy of this day of footage? I'd like to review it for the entire day."

"Sure, no problem."

He handed her a thumb drive from his shirt pocket.

"You just carry those around?" I asked with a laugh.

"Actually, yeah, just in case. They're really handy."

Jenn downloaded the footage, then handed him back the drive.

"Anything else?" she asked.

He looked at Vivian.

"I just need to know who is doing this and that I'm safe." She frowned.

"We are doing the best we can. I will ask for extra patrols to monitor your house."

"Thank you, Detective."

"Well, I'm going to get this back to the station and review it. I will have our best staff on it." He exited the office, and I watched as he walked through to the back door.

"Do you trust him?" Vivian asked me.

I thought about her question for a minute. I wanted to. Though I had a distrust of most police officers from the time I was a young child, and my father had been arrested. But there was something about the detective that made me want to believe him, want to trust him, and get to know him better.

"I do."

"Okay. Good." She nodded. "Ready to go?"

"Yes. Thanks, Jenn." I waved as we left the office.

"Anytime, Chef. See ya tomorrow."

We headed back to my house. She pulled to the curb.

"Thanks, Jess. I hope we can figure this out soon. I want to feel safe again."

"Call me anytime. I'm here for you."

I jogged up the couple of steps to the townhouse. I was so happy that we still had time for our pizza and movie night.

"Hey, how'd it go?" Sawyer asked when I came in.

"Nothing. We found the receipt, but the footage was during a busy time. It was hard to say who we were looking for."

"Bummer. But we will get this person. I promise."

"Pizza and a movie?"

"Yes!"

Chapter Nine

Two days later, we had a plan to go to Earl's apartment. I called his roommate, Silas. I lost sleep trying to come up with an excuse to talk to him. Even when I had made the call, I still had no idea what I was going to say. I figured I would just wing it.

He surprised me when he didn't ask a lot of questions.

"Earl looked up to you. I think he would want you to have his cookbooks and knife set. His mom didn't want it, so I'm glad you are coming by."

"Oh, yeah, thanks. He had mentioned the cookbooks to me many times," I lied since he gave me the idea. "I was hoping to get those."

After work, Sawyer and Vee were going with me for moral support. I didn't think Silas was a threat, but I'd never done anything like this. I thought it might ease my mind to have back up support.

I headed straight to the shower like I normally do, then got on my jeans and t-shirt. It was an old concert shirt for a local garage band that was no longer together. They thought they would be the next big alt rock band. They were good but seeing as the three of us were often the only ones at their concerts, it really wasn't a surprise.

I shook out my hair to let it air dry and then added a touch of mascara and tinted lip gloss. Nothing fancy, but I felt put together.

After work, I wouldn't usually put on make-up at all, but I thought for this mission, it was a good idea. Perhaps giving me a fake confidence.

I was ready and waiting on the couch with Lulu purring by my side when Sawyer and Vee got home.

"Welcome home." I yelled from the couch.

"Hey, oh look at you all dressed and ready." Vee said, plopping down next to me with a heavy sigh. "So tired today."

"Busy day at the post office?"

"Girl, you don't even know. It isn't even holiday season yet."

"Well, it is almost Mother's Day," I pointed out.

"That's not usually a big postal thing. I mean, I guess a lot of greeting cards, but these are all packages and stuff."

"Um, well, I don't know."

Sawyer went straight to the kitchen and came back with a glass of water.

"Was she telling you how busy it was? Crazy. I guess late tax stuff?"

"Maybe a full moon," I said.

We all shrugged in unison. Who knew?

"How are things at the restaurant?"

"Weird."

"What do you mean?" Sawyer asked as he sat down.

"It could take a bit to explain, do y'all want to change first?"

"I don't want to move for a few minutes," Vee said. She was now face down on the couch.

"Alrighty," I shrugged. "I guess, weird because I don't know what to think. We are swamped busy, but everyone comes in asking about Earl and then the shooting. I mean, I love the increase in business, but what happens when this story is old news? Do I lose all my business, or will I have loyal customers?"

"Um, interesting thought. I guess you won't know until this drama fades."

"Yeah." I groaned.

We all sat in silence for a few minutes. That's one thing I loved about us, we could just be quiet together and words weren't always necessary. It was comforting, like a warm hug.

Sawyer stood up. "I'm going to change so we can get going. Maybe if we solve this thing, it will save your business."

Vee remained face down on the couch. I leaned over to rub her shoulders and neck a little.

"Thanks." She mumbled. "I'm getting up in just one more minute. I almost promise."

"That's fine. I understand being on your feet all day."

She lifted her head. "I know you get it."

She moaned, pushing up to a seated position. I turned back to my cell phone, scrolling through social media. This was the only way I could keep up with most of my friends and family. Otherwise, I had no idea. I was too busy with my restaurant.

I stopped scrolling when I saw that my mom had posted new family pictures.

Gee, thanks, mom. I thought I was part of the family, too.

But nope, it was her and Samuel with my two bratty half-brothers. They were twenty and eighteen now, but they didn't do anything. Neither had a job and weren't in college. They just lived at home and mom waited on them all day.

I kept them at arm's length, only interacting with them for holidays or birthdays. Other than that, I rarely spoke to them. Though, yes, I tortured myself by following them on social media. Well, mom only.

Sometimes Samuel would call me, giving me a lecture about not coming around or not calling my mother. It rarely went well.

"If she acted like *my mother*, not just Bryan's and Christopher's, then maybe I would."

"Don't sass me like that, young lady."

"I'm a grown woman now, *Samuel*."

Things usually went downhill from there.

It was the same argument over and over. You'd think he would get over it and just leave me alone? I wasn't going to have a healthy relationship with them. I had a better relationship with my Grandmother Ines and my Aunt Rita.

Sawyer came down. He was wearing the same concert shirt. He saw that I was wearing it when he came home.

"Did you do that on purpose?"

"Yep! Twins."

"This is why people called us weirdos when we were in school."

"Yeah, I didn't care then and don't care now."

Vee came down a moment later in the same shirt.

"Are we ready, weirdos?" She laughed.

"I love y'all!" I laughed. They were the *best* friends. "Let's go."

Sawyer grabbed his keys. "I'll drive!"

Vee hopped in the back seat because I was much taller than her and she fit better in the back seat. Sawyer and I were both tall, so unless Vee was driving, she was in the back. We had been doing it for so long. We didn't have to talk about it. It was just natural for her to head straight for the back seat.

Silas and Earl lived in an apartment building on the opposite side of town from us. Earl liked that it was close to where he'd grown up. His mother still lived in their home from childhood, so it meant he had been closer to her. We lived near downtown which was roughly fifteen minutes by car.

I gave Sawyer directions.

"Yikes, this is not a great part of town." Sawyer said, turning right onto Cartwright Road. He hit the door lock button.

"We grew up in this part of town." Vee corrected.

It might be the poorer part of town, but her family had lived there once upon a time. They had been one of the more well-off families, but her parents were frugal. They liked to live well under their means and pinch pennies. Her father said it was why he was so rich.

"Kids, remember this, he who buys what he doesn't need, is only stealing from himself. Or herself." He told us once.

I took that to heart when I started saving for my restaurant. Don't get me wrong, I still bought things I liked. Mostly I supported many of the local artists. I loved all things art.

But their status was also one of the many things that made Vee stand out in school and why she was often labeled a weirdo with Sawyer and me.

"Yeah, so I speak from a place of experience."

"It's that place on the left." I pointed.

It was a dark red brick four story building. Some of the windows were covered in newspaper or sheets. This is where my mom lived right after my dad was sentenced to life in prison. She had stopped paying for our house, which was two blocks down and one block over. I have driven by the house as an adult. It was a tiny thing, but as a young child, it felt like a mansion.

This apartment building held haunting memories. I was reminded of my mother crying uncontrollably for hours. Me begging for food, answers, or love. It was one of the reasons I ended up spending most of my life with my grandmother.

As we exited the car to head inside, I took a deep breath and called up some inner strength.

"Flashbacks?" Vee said, coming up next to me. She knew my history and my triggers.

"Yeah, but I'm fine."

It had only been a few years before she met Samuel, and they moved to just outside of Dashwood. It wasn't exactly a suburb of

Dashwood, but sort of. It was just a neighborhood of single-family homes that sprang up to the east of downtown. The houses have large yards and lots of trees. Their mailing address was still Dashwood.

We headed in. I gagged at the smell of mold, too much garlic and spices, mixed with a strong urine smell. It hadn't changed in thirty years.

The paint was cracking and chipping off, but now it was a pale yellow instead of the olive green when we lived here. Half of the mailboxes were missing doors or open.

"Well, that's not good," Sawyer pointed. "I guess they have to come to the post office to pick up mail?"

"Maybe that's part of why we're so busy." Vee frowned.

We started up the stairs. Silas lived on four. The steps creaked and groaned as we trekked in single file up the narrow staircase.

From behind closed doors, you could hear televisions, shouting, and crying babies. Yes, more than one crying baby. I rolled my eyes. Reason one hundred and thirty-two why I didn't want children.

When we reached four, we headed to the end of the long hallway to 415. I looked at my friends as I knocked on the door.

"Coming!" Silas yelled. "Oh, hello. Come in, come in."

"Hi, Silas. Thanks for letting us come by to pick up his cookbooks and knives."

"Of course, Ole Earl would want you to have them." He gestured to the counter. "I put them in a box for you already."

"Oh, great." *Darn*. I was hoping I'd get a chance to look around.

"Is there anything else you want of his? His mom has already been here. She didn't take much, told me to just donate it, and gave me a few hundred for my trouble. Then the police have looked through his stuff, too."

"The police?"

"Yeah, said they wanted to make sure he wasn't doing anything illegal." He laughed. "Just cuz we live in this part of town, that automatically makes us criminals. Such a stereotype."

"Yeah, really? Ha ha." I felt the same way. "I assume they didn't find anything."

"You got that right. My man, Earl, was a straight-laced, wanting to stay on the right path guy. He stayed on this side of town because these are his people. His mom is here. His grandmom. You know? It's our home."

"Yeah, I know. He was a good one. I had known him since high school. I mean, I was already graduated, but I helped out at the culinary school."

"For reals? He never told me that. So y'alls go way back then."

"Yeah, we do. I'm really going to miss him." I choked on my words a bit.

Vee reached for my hand. I smiled at her.

"Well, his room is that one, feel free to look around if you want. Maybe there is a yearbook or something." He sank down onto the couch, grabbing the remote.

"Thanks."

We went to his room at the end of the hall. My first thought on entering it was he left here that day, thinking he would come back. But knowing both his mother and the police had been here, I imagine it wasn't exactly how he'd left it.

Sawyer and Vee stopped at the door, letting me walk into the room. I slowly made my way around the small space. His unmade bed was laid on the floor with no frame. His dresser with a pile of change, a couple of crumbled receipts, and a pair of sunglasses on top. A rosary was hanging on a mirror. His closet was open, showing his limited wardrobe. Like me, his clothing was either for the kitchen or for comfort.

There wasn't much to see, so I didn't know what to look for. It seemed like everything he owned was pretty much on display.

"What does a clue look like?" I whispered to my friends.

"No idea."

"Open the dresser drawers." Vee said, looking over her shoulder to make sure Silas didn't come. We didn't want to raise any eyebrows.

I opened the top drawer to reveal socks and underwear. I dug around to make sure that was it, and it was. The next drawer was empty except for a book.

"The Outsiders?" I picked it up.

I loved this book as a kid. I flipped through the pages to see if anything was stuck in it or to look for notes. A bank statement fell out of it.

I hesitated a moment, looking around the room. I half expected Earl to come in to bust me for snooping. That was silly.

I looked at the statement.

Holy crap. That was a lot of digits.

Well, it was only five digits, but still, not what I expected from him, especially seeing as his bed was on the floor. He was such a simple guy, but perhaps he was like me, saving most of his earnings.

Was he killed for money? His mom probably got that upon his death. Perhaps that is what the threat was about? Maybe this Fern person knew he had a hefty bank account.

She was who I suspected left the note on Vivian's car window, but I couldn't prove it. At least not yet. I hoped to find something.

I stared at it for a moment while I tried to decide if I should keep this for evidence or put it back. The right thing was to put it back, so I slipped it back into his book and kept looking.

The last drawer had a few ball caps in it, but nothing else. I flipped them over just to make sure there wasn't anything hiding.

Getting bolder, I grabbed a few of the receipts from on top of his dresser. Opening the first, I saw it was from the grocery store. One from Roasted Beans and one from Heroes and Villains Comics shop.

Dang it. Nothing useful.

Next, I went to his closest and thumbed through his clothes. Feeling even more confident in my snooping, I stuck my hands into some of the pants' pockets, thinking maybe a note or something would be stuck there.

Most were empty but when I tried a pair of blue jeans, I came up with a phone number with the name Flora written on it.

"Does this look like the handwriting on that note?" I handed it to my friends.

"Maybe?"

"Are you thinking this is the same girl?"

"Yeah. I mean who hasn't given a fake name a time or two." I said.

"I know I have." Sawyer chuckled.

"I haven't." Vee looked at us offended.

"You should. Lots of creeps out there." Sawyer smiled.

"I'm going to take it. Not like he needs it any longer." I shoved it into my pocket. I'd compare it when we got home.

"I guess that's it though. Nothing else here to look at. He was a simple guy." Except for nearly $40,000 in the bank. You think you know a person, but then you dig up a secret.

I looked around once more before going back into the living room area to find Silas.

"Thanks, Silas. Is this the box?" I asked, pointing to one on the kitchen counter. Even though he'd gestured to it earlier, I wanted to make sure.

"Yep, that's the one."

"Great. Oh, one question, did Earl have a girlfriend?"

"Ha, ha, funny. No, our guy was all about work and making that money. He rarely dated."

"That's what I thought."

"Why ya askin'?"

"Someone stopped by claiming to be his girlfriend. I figured she was fishing for a story or something." I tried to say it half annoyed and half like it's no big deal.

"Some girls." He chuckled as he rolled his eyes. "Probably one he had turned down. The ladies around here all wanted him because our man was going places, and that place was up." He sighed. "I can't believe he's not comin' back. I keep expecting him to come waltzing in after work with a smile or a joke, but he is gone."

"Yeah." I didn't know what else to say.

It was on the tip of my tongue to ask him about the bank account, but it didn't seem like the right thing to ask a roommate.

"Well, if you need anything else, give me a call."

I nodded. Sawyer grabbed the box for me.

"Take care. Thanks again." I said as we stepped out into the hallway.

Back in the car, I pulled the scrap of paper out of my pocket.

"I think there was a Flora that applied for a position at the restaurant." I mumbled.

"Do you remember her?"

"Not really. I don't think we actually interviewed her, but it was nearly a year ago, so I just can't remember. We could have. There were so many interviews last year as we geared up, they all blurred together."

"We remember."

They had mentioned to me often that they were worried about me. I had put in a lot of hours.

"I'm going to compare this to the handwriting on that receipt we have."

"Good idea."

"Well, not to change the subject, but what's for dinner?" Sawyer asked.

Vee and I laughed.

"You always think about food." Vee teased him.

"I can't help it. I love food. That's why one of my best friends is a chef."

"I was your best friend before I was a chef."

"True, but why do you think I kept you around?" He chuckled.

"Because, like us, you couldn't make other friends." Vee laughed.

"Okay, true again. But, seriously, dinner?"

"Stop at the store and I'll make us something. I don't know what yet, but something."

Chapter Ten

Once I had gotten home yesterday from Earl's old apartment, I had cooked for my roommates and then compared the handwriting on the receipt to the note in Earl's pants.

The phone number and name weren't much to go on. Plus, I wasn't a handwriting expert, but it did look like it could be the same, at least close enough for me to want to look up this Flora person.

I got to work early so I could look through the old resumes. I was surprised to find no cars in our parking lot. I had expected Noah to be here, but I guess I beat him.

Since I wasn't working nights any longer, I was sleeping better. That meant I was getting up refreshed and earlier.

As I made my way inside, I turned off the alarm and reset it to alert on door entry. I turned on the lights. It was quiet, almost creepy, without employees here and all the equipment turned off.

The kitchen always took my breath away a little bit. I own this. All of this! I had saved for years so that I only had to take out a small loan to get started.

I did a little twirl on my way to the office.

Once in the office, I dropped my purse into the usual desk drawer, then turned the computer on and the printer. Might as well get Noah started for the day.

Next, I went to the filing cabinet to grab the resumes, but it looked like most of them were missing. Yesterday we had well over a hundred, and now there were barely ten resumes.

"What the bleep?" I pulled them out, flipping through them. Yeah, maybe fifteen at most.

Frantically, I started opening other drawers in the file cabinet, but only found tax information, payroll information, and other business documents. No resumes.

Next, I started sifting through the desk. There wasn't much in the way of paper on the desk, so it took only a minute, but I came up empty-handed. Not even one resume.

"Well, bleepity, bleep, bleep." I slammed my hands down as I scanned the room trying to think of where they could be.

I heard the door open and the alarm sound, but before I could duck and cover, it went off. I stuck my head around the corner of the office.

"Hello?"

"Jess?" It was Noah. "Why are you here so early?"

"Just looking for a resume. Did you move them?"

"No, in the top drawer, in alphabetical order."

"Nope. It seems like most are missing. Only about 15 are here."

He came over to look, then did a double take looking around the room, and then pulled the drawer open again.

"Well, son of a—" He looked at me. "Where did they go?"

"Maybe Jenn has them for some reason." I shrugged.

"I'll call her." He took out his cell phone. I could only hear his side of the conversation, but it didn't sound like she knew either. He hung up and looked at me. "I am as stumped as you. I swear they were just here. Didn't you, Vivian, and Detective Upton look through them just the other day?"

"Yeah, and Jenn was here. We left them with her."

"Yeah, and she left them for me to put away. I love her, but she isn't as organized as … well, as I like to be." He laughed.

He was a special kind of organizer. Nobody I knew was like Noah. That's why I liked him.

"Should we check the security footage for the office?" I suggested.

"Oh, good idea. I always forget that one is in here."

"I hope you aren't doing anything embarrassing while you're alone." I teased.

"Of course not." He sounded offended.

He typed into the computer bringing the cameras up. It took a moment to load. He selected the office one rewinding to the last moment we knew they were here. Then he did a fast forward to present time. It took us roughly fifteen minutes at double speed to go through just those few days.

"Nothing, but you saw me put them in the file cabinet," Noah said.

"Yeah. Then neither of you touch them and nobody else comes in or near the cabinet."

"So, what? They just disappeared?"

I shrugged. I know magic wasn't real, but I had no explanation for where they were.

"We need to have a staff meeting anyway, so maybe we can ask if anyone knows anything?" I said.

"If someone took them, why would they fess up? Then if they knew enough to manipulate the security footage, they are definitely not going to rat themselves out, right?"

I thought about all my employees. I couldn't picture any of them doing it. Why would they? What would be the motive? I mean I got some creepy vibes from Eric, but that didn't mean he had a reason to do this.

I just couldn't figure out why or what someone could possibly want with the resumes? It didn't make sense.

"Okay, well, we still need to call a staff meeting. How about tomorrow at three? That seems to be the slowest time," I finally said.

"Alrighty. I'll call those that aren't here today to make sure they come in for it and post it on our schedule."

On the online scheduler that we used to create the weekly schedule, there was an announcement section. This would be the first time we were going to use it. I hoped it worked.

We would also go a little old school by posting it on the whiteboard outside the office and the word of mouth method.

The schedule for most employees was the same each week, but we would sometimes have an employee who was off, so someone else may help cover their shift.

"Thanks. I'll pass the word to everyone today."

"And I'll keep an eye out for those wayward resumes."

I nodded and went to get the kitchen warmed up and start my prep for the day. As each employee came in, the word was spread about the employee meeting tomorrow afternoon. I was still trying to decide what I was going to talk about, but I had planned to do this once a month, so it was time for our first.

The original plan was for it to be a pulse and morale check of the team. How was everyone doing? What could I do differently? What could the team do better? What are they hearing about the restaurant? That kind of thing.

Earl's murder was an oddity that I hope I never had to address with them again.

The next day went quickly. Now we were gathering in the bar area for our staff meeting. We had one table with two customers at it. They seemed to be having a business meeting, which meant they didn't need much. They had already eaten.

Ava simply made sure they had drinks refilled, got their bill settled, and let them know we were having a staff meeting, but she was available if they needed anything.

"Okay, thanks for joining us today for this. I'll try to keep it brief, but I just wanted to do a check in with everyone. What's working? What's not? What are you hearing? But first, I want to express my gratitude and appreciation to each and every one of you. We have had a good, but also rough, month. We lost one of our own. He will be missed, but in the wake of that, we were brought June who has been a wonderful addition. Her pimento cheese spread has been a huge hit."

"It has!" Several servers said.

"Everyone is asking for it."

"We sell out by the end of the night," one of the line cooks yelled.

"I'm so glad to hear it. Thanks, June."

"My pleasure. I feel blessed to be here, too. You don't know what it means to me to be somewhere I am wanted and appreciated." She smiled. A few of the employees sitting closest to her hugged her or patted her back.

"Alright, so now, tell me what you think *isn't* working?"

They all looked around at each other. Either nobody wanted to go first, or they didn't have anything.

"Well, this might not count," Skye started to say, "but I can't tell if people are coming in because they like the food or they want to hear drama about Earl."

I had the same thought, and if the murmurs among the staff were to be believed, everyone was thinking the same.

"I keep thinking when the news of his death slows, so will we," Parker added.

"But then I read the online reviews, and they are glowing."

"Yeah, on Yelp, we have a 4.8."

"On Google, it's a 4.9."

"Did anyone read Ms. Lynette's most recent review? She gave glowing comments about June's cheese."

"Yes!" came a chorus of voices.

Everyone started talking at once about reading this one or that online. It really sounded like people did like the food, but would it last? Maybe I just had impostor syndrome.

As we sat there talking, I saw that the front door opened. In marched Detective Upton, followed by another officer.

Well, bleep. I thought.

I stood to meet them across the room. "Just a sec, y'all."

My staff turned to watch me walk away, then the low murmurs started.

"Hello Detective Upton. Officer Rafferty." I greeted them both.

I knew Officer Rafferty from high school. We were classmates, at least until I moved to the culinary arts program. He continued on the more traditional path, but in a semi-small town, we ran into each other here and there through the years.

"Chef." Detective Upton said. "We just wanted to have a quick chat with you and show you some of the footage. We have it narrowed down to a few people. One in particular."

"Do you want to come back to the office?" I asked.

"Sure."

"Okay, give me a minute to wrap up with my staff. Would y'all like a drink?"

"I'd love one of those peach lemonades in a to-go cup if possible." The detective said.

"Maxine's iced tea in a to-go cup for me, Jess." Officer Rafferty smiled.

"Okay. I'll be back in one, maybe two minutes." I gestured for them to have a seat in a booth.

I walked over to the bar and asked Maxine to get them drinks.

"Sorry, team, I think we were getting some good discussion happening, but they need me to review some footage, so for now, it's a wrap." I checked the time. "It's almost shift change, anyway. Thank you all for everything. Your hard work and dedication to my dream has been so appreciated. I couldn't do this without each and every one of you."

They started moving chairs back into place. Maxine handed me the drinks for the officers.

"Thanks." I took a deep breath as I walked over to invite them back. "Okay, here is the lemonade, and this is the iced tea. Plus, straws."

"Thanks."

I held my hand out for the straw wrappers, then dropped them in the trash when we got to the kitchen.

Both Noah and Jenn were in the office. They greeted the officers. Officer Rafferty set down a laptop and fired it up.

"Okay, so we fast forwarded past where we had stopped viewing this the other day, and saw this," Detective Upton said as he nodded for Rafferty to hit play.

The screen came to life showing the front door and sidewalk of The Crock Pot. A few people walked through together. That was the older ladies, and I recognized June in the group.

Seconds later, a figure with a hoodie pulled up over their head and covering their face walked out. They stuck out their middle finger at the camera without looking at it and kept walking.

"Well, that was rude." Noah huffed.

"Yeah, little bit." I frowned.

"Any idea on who it might be?" Detective Upton asked.

"No, none. Either of you?" I looked at Noah and Jenn.

"Not a clue."

"Nope, doesn't look familiar, but hard to tell with their face covered."

"Well, that leads us to the next question. Do you have different camera angles? Like from inside that maybe we could compare this to."

"Yeah, one is pointing at the front door, then one is wide, but it is mostly focused back towards the kitchen area doors. Just in case anyone comes from the kitchen. Then we have one in the bar, the back door and a wide view of the kitchen."

"And don't forget the one in here." Noah said, turning to wave at it.

"Ha, yes, that one, too." I pointed at it.

The officers both looked. I didn't mention that we had concerns about the reliability of that camera or any of the cameras, but it was all we had.

"Can you show us the front door?" Upton asked.

Jenn was closest to our computer, so she pulled it up, clicking until she selected the interior one facing the front door.

"Here."

"Is this right now?"

"Yes but let me back it up. What date and time was it again?"

Rafferty told her, so she clicked to just a minute or so before. The ladies left and then a second later, the person in the dark hoodie walked out, head turned away from the camera as if they knew it was there. Not that it was hidden exactly. But I didn't go into places and look for the cameras. I just assumed they were there.

"Okay, can you try the wide angle facing the kitchen?"

She clicked until she found the right camera at the same date and time.

Again, as with the other footage, we see the ladies' group standing from their table in the middle of the restaurant. The other person is not visible at all, though there seems to be a slight black blur from the side.

"They must have been in one of those front tables," Noah said.

It was that same chick.

"It has to be that Fern chick, but I don't know her real name."

"Did you look back through the resumes again?" Upton asked.

Noah, Jenn, and I exchanged a look. We knew those had disappeared.

"Wait, what was that look?" He asked.

"Sometime after you, Vivian, and I went through them, they disappeared."

"Disappeared?"

"Well, I filed them back into the file cabinet that next morning. We saw it on our camera, but then when Jess went to look for one yesterday, they were gone."

"Gone?"

"Yeah, gone." What part of that was he having a hard time with? I gave him the benefit of the doubt that he was just as shocked by their disappearance as we were.

"Can we see that footage?"

"Sure." Jenn did her magic again. She pointed out that Noah had them all and then hit fast forward at a slow enough speed that you could tell what was going on, but not so slow that it took forever. "And now see, this is yesterday morning."

It shows me looking for them and then looking around, confused. Then Noah came in and joined in the search.

"We need to get our digital forensic team on this," Upton said to Rafferty.

"Do you think it was hacked or something?" I asked.

"Yes."

"And can they … um, fix it?" I wasn't sure what the right terminology was for that.

"I honestly don't know." He rubbed his chin. He was clean shaven most of the time, but today there was a bit of stubble. "We will have someone contact you. They may need access to your network, IP address, and other stuff. I don't know. I'm not hugely technical either."

"Okay, no problem. We are happy to help."

"Great. And one question, is there anyone on your staff that could have done this?"

Jenn and I gasped, but Noah smirked a bit. That was his thought exactly.

"I just can't even imagine any of them doing it," I said.

"Well, alrighty." He made a note in a small notepad. "That is all we need. We will keep working. Thank you. Oh, and thank you for the drinks. This is my new favorite thing."

"Mine too." Rafferty said, as he took another big sip.

"I'll walk you both out," Noah offered.

I plopped hard into a chair and stared at Jenn.

"I knew there was a possibility the footage had been tampered with, but I didn't want to believe it. I really kept thinking that maybe we just misplaced them somehow."

Though that many seemed so unlikely to be misplaced, and I knew they couldn't sprout legs and walk off on their own. That left someone taking them. Someone on my staff. It shook me to my core.

"I know." She looked around, then lowered her voice. "Do you think it could be one of the employees?"

Could she read minds? But I really couldn't picture anyone doing it.

"I really don't. Whoever that Fern chick is, that's who we need to be looking for."

"I think you're right."

But without her real name, I didn't know how I would find her. It was like a needle in a haystack.

Chapter Eleven

Yesterday had not been a great day. Detective Upton and Officer Rafferty had confirmed my worst fear. Even if I wanted to live in denial, we had a mole in our building.

Now I was side eyeing everyone on the staff, even my most trusted employees, like Noah and Jenn. They had keys to the safe and knew all the financial ins and outs.

However, they seemed as confused about the resumes and footage as I was. We sat for an hour going through everything. We tore up the office, looking in every place that paper could go in the building. Nothing.

But today, I would have the whole day off. I couldn't wait. It had been more than a month without a break. I was nearing burnout.

June was now fully acclimated and ready to be in charge. Plus, I had Parker to work with her on the day shift, and then Stelly would help her on the evening shift.

"Are you sure you are ready for a full day? It is long." I had asked June.

"Oh, please, Chef. I might be old, but I don't feel my age."

"Well if, you're sure."

"Go. Take a most deserved and earned day off."

So, for the first time in a long time, I slept in. Once I was awake, I moved from my bed to the couch. I snuggled into my blanket with the remote, a cup of coffee, and my Lulu cat. She had never been a huge snuggler, but I guess absence makes the heart grow fonder. Anytime I was home now, she would follow me around and if I sat or laid down, she was on me meowing.

Once Sawyer and Vee got home, the plan was to go looking for this Fern person. I had no idea where to even start, but they had some ideas.

I dozed on the couch and woke up when a 6 foot 4-inch-tall Sawyer jumped on me with a laugh.

"Dude!" I yelled, punching him playfully.

"No sleeping." He laughed as he punched me back. Neither hit the other hard. It was just playful taps. "We're going to change and then we want to get this party rolling out."

"Fine, okay. I'm going." I stretched, yawned, then pushed off the couch for the first time all day. It had been nice to not move for hours.

I headed straight to my bathroom. We each had our own, plus there was a half bathroom on the first floor. It was a perfect roommate house, and that's what the landlord had advertised it as.

The management company had a block of eight townhouses. They took care of all external maintenance and any general issues. It was the ideal for us.

We hadn't met many of our neighbors. Strike that. I hadn't, but Sawyer, the social butterfly, had met all of them. He would often have coffee with the ladies in 1408. They were two doors down and had a front porch on their unit, and he would sit out there for hours gossiping and chatting with them. It was adorable, but I couldn't do it.

They had invited me before and after half an hour, I was squirming in my chair from boredom. It wasn't that they weren't interesting. In fact, they had forty years of experience on us, and a passport full of stamps. They were fun to talk to in short bouts.

My problem was I was used to moving a lot and sitting for long periods of time, except for today, often left me fidgeting and ready to move. Today was an anomaly for me.

I pulled on black jeans, a graphic t-shirt with a hot pink skull and knives. When I paired this with my beat-up black tennis shoes, it was a look for sure. I had never been one of those girly-girl types, preferring black and gray over colors and frills. That didn't in and of itself make me not girly, but I just didn't care about how I looked.

Perhaps it was because of my size, I felt as if frilly things looked like a tent on me. Oversized t-shirts and jeans worked fine, and got the job done. Since I spent most of my time in a hot kitchen, my chef clothes were of much more importance to me.

"Ready, Jessie?" Vee yelled.

"Yeah, I'm coming." I grabbed my purse, a black hobo bag because it held everything I needed, then jogged down the stairs, jumping the last few steps. "Here."

"You're goofy. I have missed you," she said, hugging me.

Vee was a hugger. She had been like that since we were in middle school. At first, I hated it. I had not been in an affectionate family. Even before my father went to prison and my parents were happily married, there weren't hugs and kisses between them or from them to me.

Vee came from a happier childhood that she was always trying to rebel against with no luck. Her family was close and functional, so what could she do? Hug me.

Sawyer was already standing by the door.

"Your taxi awaits." He laughed, opening the door for us.

We scrambled down the steps. The music blasted us when he turned on the car.

"Ack, sorry, we were jamming on the way home. I forgot to turn it down."

"So, what's the plan?" I asked as he pulled away from the curb. He seemed to have one.

"Well, I was asking around in the mailroom. Just to see if any of the carriers had seen someone with her description." He paused as he checked his blind spot before changing lanes. He was the safest driver I knew, and why he was normally the driver in our group. "Larry said that he saw someone like her over at Inked It. Though he said he wasn't sure if she was a customer or worked there."

Inked It was a tattoo shop that we all loved. It was the best in Dashwood. Though with a town of artists, you couldn't go wrong with most of them.

"Really? They all have colored hair, so that's not a stretch."

"Well, it's all I got, so we were heading there."

"Alright. I might ask Stevie about another tattoo while we're there."

I studied the one on my forearm. It was a reminder of my alphabet soup. It was a steaming pot with a few letters floating. It was about 2 inches tall by an inch wide, so not overly large, but a good reminder of where I came from.

I have one on my left shoulder blade of crossed chef knives. I initially wanted to get one in honor of opening The Crock Pot, but now I was thinking of something to honor Earl, but I didn't know what yet.

"I should get one, too," Vee said from the backseat.

She was the only one of us that didn't yet have one. I argued that if she didn't have one by now, she never would. She would say it was because she hadn't decided on what to get yet.

"Your mother would kill you," I teased.

"Oh, please," she laughed, but then said, "I would just get it where she can't see it."

I laughed. Vee was so … well Vee.

"You want so badly to be a bad girl like me, don't you?" I turned to look at her.

"I'm bad."

"At cooking," I said.

"At singing." Sawyer added.

"Hey, y'all are mean."

"Are we lying?" Sawyer teased.

"No, but you don't have to point it out." She crossed her arms and stared out the window. She wasn't truly mad. This was just us.

I turned back around as we neared the tattoo shop. As we drove down the block, there was no parking in front. Sawyer drove down the block and back up, managing to find a spot across the street in a small parking lot next to the comic book shop, Heroes and Villains Comics.

"Remind me, I need to stop in there," Vee said.

"Why? Ricky moved away," Sawyer said.

"Not because of him. That ended a long time ago."

"Then why?"

"That new Pop Funko figurine I wanted came out. I need to pick it up."

"Oh, boy." I rolled my eyes.

It was cute, really, and made it fairly easy to buy for her. I didn't collect anything, but she had been collecting these figures forever. She had them lining her walls. I couldn't let Lulu go into her room because she would knock them over.

When Lulu was a kitten, she knocked them all over while we were all working. Vee nearly had a heart attack when she came home to find her beloved collectables on the floor. It took two more times before it was agreed upon that Lulu was not allowed in and Vee would keep her door shut.

We got out of the car and carefully made our way to the shop. Stepping inside the tattoo shop, it smelled like incense, rubbing alcohol, and too much body spray.

"Hey, Chef!" Stevie yelled from across the shop. She had a man face down on her table, and she was working on his back. At this angle, I couldn't tell what it was, but it took up most of his back. "One, sec, hun." She said to the man, putting down her tattoo gun, peeling her gloves off, and walking to us.

She gave me an elbow bump in greeting.

"What can I do for you?"

I looked around. I didn't see any employees that I didn't already know. There was Snake, Lucas, and Talia.

"Do you know someone with purple and black hair about this tall?" I held my hand up at about five feet five inches, give or take. "She might go by the name Fern, but we don't think that's her real name."

"Um, maybe. Is it to her shoulder?"

"Yeah, all one length, straight."

"Flora." Snake came over to say. "Her name is Flora. I just did a tat on her last week."

"Oh, that one with the rosebud and sword?" Stevie looked at him.

"Yeah, that one." Snake chuckled. "That girl is wacky."

"Why do you say that?" Sawyer asked.

"She was talking about all this conspiracy theory stuff. Mumbling about how she was going to make things right." Snake looked at Stevie. "Do you remember her saying that?"

"Yeah, but it was all jumbled up and didn't make sense."

"Did she mention me at all?" I asked.

"You? Why would she?" Stevie looked confused.

"She seems to have a problem with me, and I'm just trying to find her so I can find out why."

"Now that you mention it, she was talking about a restaurant and *that* chef, though she didn't name names," Snake said. "I guess that could be you, but we have lots of restaurants and lots of chefs."

"Do you remember anything else she said?"

"That's it. Like I said, most of it was just nonsense about seeking revenge to those in power."

"You didn't think that was alarming?"

"We get all types in here. Mostly regular people, but I gave a tat to someone last week that kept talking about the alien overlords coming soon. His tattoo was a symbol he claimed tagged him as a believer." Talia added from behind us. "And that wasn't even the worst of what I've heard."

"Yeah, some people use us as therapy." Stevie laughed.

"Kinda like bartenders or hairstylists. We hear stuff," Talia said.

I looked at my friends who were just standing there listening. I shrugged, and they did as well.

"Well, thanks, y'all. That's helpful." Even though I wasn't sure if it was, at least we had her real first name.

We stepped outside. I felt frustrated and vulnerable. It was a bit unsettling that they heard such things and didn't bat an eye over it. That either was a good or bad thing, but at the moment, I couldn't decide which it was.

It wasn't until we had left that I remembered I had wanted to ask about a new tattoo. Oh well, save that for another day.

"Time for the comic book shop." Vee squealed and made a beeline across the street. Sawyer and I laughed as we trailed behind her.

Back in school, we used to spend a lot of time here browsing comic books, reading them, and trading them. We'd spend hours playing Dungeons and Dragons, Pokémon, and various other card games.

The owner, Monte, had been a staple in the place for as long as I can remember. Walking in, the bell chimed our arrival and the smell of old paper and mold hit the same as it did twenty plus years ago. There was classic rock playing through the speakers. Monte loved the Eagles, the Who, and Led Zeppelin.

Looking around, we were the only customers currently.

"Hey, Monte, do you have my figure?" Vee said, stepping up to the counter.

"Right here." He pulled it from behind the counter.

"Oh, nice! Thanks so much. I have just the spot for him." She stared at the wizard from her favorite video game.

Sawyer and I started browsing through the boxes of comics. I hadn't read one in a few years, but I still enjoyed them. I made my way to the back wall where Monte hung local artists' works. I wish I had this talent.

As I browsed, one portrait of a demon woman pulled me in. I stepped closer to study her face.

It was haunting and beautiful, and oddly familiar. Something in her face.

"You like that one?" A voice behind me said.

I turned to find Fern or Flora or whatever her name was, standing there. I looked at her and at the painting.

"Is this you?"

"Yes," she snapped. "A self-portrait, sort of."

"It's stunning."

"Thank you." she said, tight-lipped. "What are you doing here?"

"My friend had something ordered, so came to pick it up."

"Umph."

"What is your problem with me?"

"You don't know?"

"No."

"You didn't hire me. Didn't even give me a chance." She stared at her picture, not making eye contact with me as she spoke.

"I didn't hire a lot of people, but they don't flip off my security cameras, try to steal Earl's check, or shoot at me."

"Shoot at you? Ha, not me, honey." She rolled her head around to face me more fully. "The other two things, yeah, I did because you are a fake chef wannabe and people need to know."

"That's doesn't explain why you tried to take his check," I crossed my arms. I ignored the fake chef part, because I had won enough cooking competitions to not take her opinion seriously.

"I took a chance. Can you blame me? Free money if you fell for it."

"Um, well, it's stealing."

"Like I care. If you would have believed me, I wouldn't have gotten caught. He is dead so who would know?"

I didn't know what to say to that. She took a step forward. My heartbeat quickened. I wasn't one to fight, even if I was nearly a foot taller and easily had 80 pounds on her.

"It's okay though. You aren't all that, and I'm going to expose you." She snickered and then walked away.

"Hey, wait a sec?"

She turned slowly, her face red. "What?"

"What the heck is your name? It's not Fern."

"Ha, you don't even know." She turned to leave again. "Check the picture," she threw over her shoulder as she went out the door.

I looked at the picture and saw the signature. It was scrolled in bright dripping red paint. Flora.

Well, at least I knew for certain that was her name. Same as the name on the note in Earl's pocket and what they said at Inked It.

Lot of good it did since I didn't have most of the resumes, but at least one mystery was solved. I had her name, phone, and now knew she hated me simply for not hiring her.

I could live with that, but if she wasn't the one that shot at me, who was? Plus, how was she connected to Earl? Why did he have her phone number?

I did a mental facepalm. I should have just called the number, but honestly, I had assumed it was fake until that minute. Perhaps I would try it later if I really wanted to know her problem.

For now, I will let it go. It was enough to know her real name.

Chapter Twelve

When I arrived at work the next day, I went straight to the office to look through the files just to see if one of the remaining resumes had the name Flora on it. Opening the drawer, my eyes almost bugged out of my head.

I picked up the files.

"They're all here," I said out loud.

All the resumes were returned, or so it seemed. I couldn't remember how many we had before, but the stack seemed about this thick.

What the heck?

Someone was seriously trying to mess with my mind. That was the only explanation I had for this. It made no sense to take and return the resumes.

I fired up the computer, then clicked over to the security footage, fast forward through the last 24 hours. Nothing unusual. This was the strangest thing ever.

I would need to get this other footage to the detective so that his team could review it as well. Though I hadn't heard anything about the other footage yet, and I probably wouldn't.

I also needed to find my own cybersecurity person. Someone that could check this footage and tell if or how it was edited, because I knew it had to have been.

Noah came into the office.

"What's wrong?"

"How—"

"Your face says it all." He pointed to the pile in front of me. "Wait, are those the missing resumes?"

"Yeah, can you believe it? I was checking the security footage. Just like last time. Nothing. I was trying to see if I could tell where it was sliced or edited or whatever the term is."

"Has the detective called?"

"No, I need to call him now that these have shown up again."

I flipped through them, looking for Flora's name, finding the name Flora Jackson. Wait? Jackson, could she be the daughter of the man my father killed?

"Bleepity-bleep." I started typing into the search engine: ***Tito Vasquez murder trial***.

"What are you looking for?" Noah came to look over my shoulder.

"The name of the man my father killed all those years ago. His last name was Jackson. Could this Flora be the baby his wife was pregnant with at the time?"

"Dang."

I clicked on some of the old news stories. I read the facts that I already knew.

Martin Jackson was shot to death by Tito Vasquez witnessed by his daughter Jessica Vasquez, age 5. Martin leaves behind a pregnant wife and a young son.

I clicked through a few more articles, but nothing that gives a name for either child. Makes sense, as one wasn't born, and the other was a minor.

But they listed my name, I thought. Seeing as my dad committed the crime, I supposed we didn't get the same level of privacy. I had also been a witness, not that I remembered much about the details.

I sighed and looked up at Noah.

"I guess it's possible that she is his daughter," Noah said.

"Yeah." I clicked to close the browser. "I talked to her yesterday."

"You did? How? What did you say? Where?" He rapidly fired the questions at me.

"At the comic bookstore."

"Comic books?"

"My roommate collects those pop figures."

"Ah, and?"

"And she said I didn't hire her, so she was going to expose me or something like that."

"Didn't hire her?" He blurted. "We didn't hire a bunch of people."

"I know, that's what I said."

He started reading her resume, and the attached application. He pulled a notebook out of his desk, flipped through several pages, and then stopped.

"Here she is." He pointed. "We didn't hire her because she wasn't qualified to cook. She had no training for that, but we offered her a runner or busser position. She turned those down."

"Well, so it wasn't just that we didn't hire her, but not for the position she wanted."

"Yeah."

"Everyone thinks they can cook. I mean, she probably can at home with all the time in the world, but in a fast-paced kitchen, it's different. Plus, everyone starts somewhere." I rubbed my temples.

A headache was forming, and I still had to work my shift. Today I would work from opening until closing so June could be off. We were still trying to figure out the best schedule so that we could each have time off.

I was also going to work more with Parker to get him trained. The plan was for him to be a sous chef that could run the kitchen when June and I weren't around. Three chefs were better than one.

I hadn't yet figured out if it would be Stelly or Hannah who would then step into his role as the lead line cook. Perhaps each of them could be one on day and one on night shift.

Noah pulled out the sales from the night before. We reviewed those and went through our inventory report. Then, he would be putting in a food order, so I went through that so I could approve it.

"Alright, I guess I need to get my station prepped." I nodded to Noah.

A few hours later, Eric came into the kitchen. Eric was one of our runners and filled in as busser, dishwasher, and most anything else we needed around the restaurant, except for cooking.

"Chef, the detective is here eating lunch with his family, and he is asking for you."

"Really? Okay." I wiped my hands. "Parker, you good?"

"Yes, Chef."

I went to the sink to wash up and then went to the dining room. I scanned the room for the detective. That's when I saw his sweet family sitting together on the right side of the room.

They looked like any normal family. I'm not sure what I expected. Detective wife and tiny detectives with badges, shiny sunglasses, and tiny notepads, maybe? I stifled a laugh, but the image of the detective family cracked me up.

"Hi, Detective," I said as I walked up.

"Hi, Chef. This is my wife, Brooke, our son, Aiden, and daughter, Evie."

"Nice to meet you," I said. Brooke smiled as she helped Aiden with his grilled cheese. "You have a beautiful family."

"Thanks."

"How is everything?"

"Excellent. I had your alphabet soup. Fantastic." Brooke smiled.

"And the pimento cheese as an appetizer, perfect." Detective Upton added.

"Oh, yes, that was Aiden's favorite part." Brooke added. "Wasn't it, buddy?"

He grinned around his grilled cheese sandwich.

"I'm glad to hear it. That was a recent addition." I said, smiling. "You wanted to speak to me?"

"Yes." He looked at his wife. "One second."

She nodded.

He pushed himself to the edge of the booth. "Can we speak over by the bar, maybe?"

"Absolutely."

We walked over to the end of the bar, where it was quiet. Ripley deposited a peach lemonade for me with a wink. My staff really took care of me. I appreciate each and every one of them.

"So, what's up?" I asked once we were seated at the bar.

"Well, so far, the edited footage hasn't shown anything, but the forensic team is working on it. We might have narrowed down the person of interest on your security camera."

"I actually found her and talked to her."

"You did?"

"Yes, yesterday I was off and was out with my roommates. We made a stop at Heroes and Villains comic bookstore, and there she was. Flora Jackson is her name."

He pulled out his tiny notepad and scribbled it down. The image of the detective family popped in my head again. A giggle nearly escaped, but I swallowed it.

"Okay, good. I'll see if I can talk to her. Get an alibi for the night Earl was shot and then for the day that you and his mom were shot at."

"Thanks. Wait? Is that the name you had?"

"Yes, actually, but wrote down that you identified her as the same person."

"Ah, okay." I nodded. "Also, I was going to call you later. The missing resumes showed up. Just found them this morning."

"Really? That's strange."

"It is. There didn't seem to be any missing, but we didn't have a good record of exactly how many we had. It's just a guess. Noah and I reviewed the security footage, and again, nothing shows."

"Can I get a copy of that as well?"

"Of course. Noah already has it on a USB. We can go back and get it, but anything else?"

"We found a few cars that matched the description you gave of the car that shot at you, but none with paper plates. They all had regular plates. This thing is so frustrating." He sighed. "But I just wanted to tell you, or warn you, that the Chief is putting a lot of pressure on us to get this resolved. He is hinting that he wants to bring you in again for another round of questions."

"But I didn't do it. I mean, you can see that on the security footage, right? I walk up and find him."

"I know, I know." He put his hands up in defeat. "But he seems to have a thorn in his side about it. Even if we brought you in, he can't make it stick, so please don't fret too much about it. I really just wanted you to know, so you weren't caught off guard if it happened."

"Thank you so much. I haven't had a lot of trust for law enforcement, considering my history." I blushed.

"I'm familiar."

"Oh, speaking of that, Flora Jackson. Jackson was the last name of the man my father … well, you know. She looks to be about the right age to have been the child his wife was pregnant with." I left my thoughts open-ended to see if he would pick up what I was thinking.

"I will look into that. Could be motive for her to shoot at you, perhaps."

Glad he got that without me saying it.

"Thanks. Let's go get you that USB drive."

I grabbed my lemonade to take with us as we went to the office. He nodded to several of the staff members as we walked back.

He stopped just as we made it into the kitchen.

"I'm always so impressed with how your staff just seems to know what to do. You know, like when you are watching birds flying together and they seem to instinctively know which way the leader is going." He stopped to watch them for a moment, so I took a second to take them all in with him.

It was true. The ticket printed and one of the line cooks would call out the order, then everyone worked to get the dishes plated and out. The runners and servers would come collect the plates, while the bussers brought back the dirty things. From there, the dishwashers took over, just for it to start all over again.

It was a symphony in motion, or like he said, a flock of birds flying together.

"Knock, knock," I said at the door of the office. "Detective Upton is here for that USB."

"Hello, Detective," Noah said, standing. He grabbed the USB from the desk. "I added a few extra days to it, so it is three days' worth of footage. Just in case there is anything nefarious that we missed."

"Thanks for this. That will help. I will get it to the team right away."

"I'll walk you out," I offered.

"Thanks. If either of you find anything out, don't hesitate to call me." He looked at me when he said that, even though he was addressing us both.

"We will," we both confirmed.

I walked him back to his table, where his son was smiling with a dish of chocolate and banana pudding. It came with a few tiny vanilla cookies.

"Are you enjoying that pudding?" I asked him.

He nodded his head as he spooned another spoonful in his mouth.

"Everything was excellent. We are fans," Brooke said.

"Well, thank you. We hope you will come again. I will let you finish your meal."

It was on the tip of my tongue to offer to cover their bill, but I didn't want to set a precedent and didn't want to seem like I was buying his favor. I know I'd given him a free drink before, but an entire meal was something different.

I went back to the kitchen to finish out my long day.

Chapter Thirteen

I yawned as I pulled into the parking lot, coffee in a to-go cup in the center console. Pulling into the back, I parked in my usual spot.

I made my way to the back door, but noticed a crowd was gathered near the entrance. I thought maybe they were confused, thinking we served breakfast, which we don't currently.

As I walked over to let them know, I was hit with the realization of what had happened. Someone had spray-painted on the side of the building the words killer and the word that rhythms with witch.

I gasped, and all eyes turned to me.

Then the questions started flying from the onlookers.

"Chef, do you know who would have done this?"

"Why would they write that?"

"Did you kill someone?"

"Did you kill your sous chef?"

"You need to get rid of that curse word! Think of the children."

I mumbled something, then pulled out my phone to call the detective, walking away from the crowd so I would be able to hear him.

"This is Detective Upton."

"Detective, this is Chef Jessica Vasquez at The Crock Pot. Someone vandalized the side of my restaurant. They wrote killer and a curse word."

"I'll send a patrol car and I'll be on my way shortly, too."

"Thanks."

We hung up. I took a quick picture of the damage, sending it in a group text to my friends. They were both at work already and likely wouldn't see it until later.

Next, I called Noah.

"Hey, Chef. I'm about to pull in. Is something wrong?"

"Yeah, someone spray-painted on the side of the building. The police are on their way."

"Damn. Okay, I'm a block away. I'll be there in a minute."

We hung up. A few employees showed up and joined me, staring at the spray-painted words. I have to admit; it was beautiful lettering. I had a really strong feeling about who had done this, and her name wasn't Fern.

"Oh, wow, Chef. This is not good," Noah said when he joined us. "Can we clean it?"

"I don't know yet. The police are on their way, and I am hoping we got it on camera."

We both turned to look at the camera. It was spray-painted solid black. I hadn't noticed that until just now.

"Bleepity, bleep." I muttered. "I have a feeling we aren't going to see anything leading up to this, just blackness."

"I hate to say it, but you're right," Noah said, running his hand through his hair. "I'll go check, anyway."

He turned and headed into the building via the back door. I told the rest of the employees to start getting set up for the day. We had a lot to do before lunch.

My phone chimed that I had a message. It was Sawyer.

S: Dang. You think Flora did that?

Me: Looks like her style.

S: You call the police?

Me: Y

S: Let me know what happens.

Me: Will do

I wanted to cry as I slid my phone back into my pocket. Most of the onlookers had moved on. There were a few new people now, but most looked and continued on their way. I paced around, waiting. I needed this resolved and cleaned up before lunch.

I silently cursed my prime location in town now. We had a corner lot that was situated on two high traffic roads and just a block from downtown and city hall.

Most of the town would drive by here, which you wanted so people would stop to eat. However, this morning, it was not what I wanted people to see.

The police station wasn't too far, why weren't they here yet? More employees arrived and I sent them all in to focus on work. We had a short window to get all our prepping done for the day.

Finally, a patrol car pulled to the curb next to me. Out stepped Officer Rafferty and another officer that I didn't know.

"Hey, Jess."

"Hey Raff. Thanks for coming." I pointed.

"Nice." He chuckled, then sobered when he looked at me. "Sorry to see this. You have a nice place here."

The other officer started taking pictures. I pointed out that the security camera had been tampered with, too.

"Noah went to see what footage he could get from it, but we are sure it won't be much."

"Alright. Any ideas on who?" Rafferty asked.

"Flora Jackson. She's a local artist, and she is the one that flipped off my security camera a week or so ago, and a few other things."

"Oh, I know Flora. Yeah, actually, now that you mention it, this does look like her style," Rafferty said, then cleared his throat as I gave him a death stare. "We'll look into her."

Noah came jogging out. He had a USB drive in his hand.

"Not much, but at least you can get the timing of when everything went down." He handed it to the other officer. "Maybe check some of the other business's cameras?"

Rafferty nodded. Why did I feel like we were telling him how to do his job? We were spoon feeding them clues and footage. He was a good guy, but was he just not trained well or simply bad at it?

"Can we start having Arlo clean this off?" I asked. "We have to get ready for lunch."

The two officers looked at each other, nodding as if they had a silent conversation.

"Yeah, we have enough to go on. I mean there isn't much we can do in this case besides take pictures, take a statement, and this helps." He held up the USB drive.

"Alright." Well, that was useless and frustrating, but at least we could start cleaning up the building.

As they were turning to leave, Detective Upton arrived. They waited for him to exit his car and join us. When he walked up, he whistled, taking in the scene.

"They really did a number here."

"Yeah," I said, flatly.

"Do you have pictures?" he asked the officers. They nodded. "Security footage?"

"Sort of," Noah said, pointing at the camera. "I gave them what we had."

"Well, dang," Upton said, looking at the painted camera. "Do you need help to get this cleaned up?"

"We have a pressure washer and Arlo, our custodian, can manage it." I nodded at Noah. He turned to go get Arlo.

"Alright then, since we have the security footage and the pictures, I'll leave you to it," Upton said.

"Yep, and this is classic Flora Jackson," Rafferty said.

"I needed to speak to her anyway, so I have an even better reason to bring her in for a talk."

"You haven't talked to her yet?" I had thought this was perhaps retaliation for them interviewing her already.

"Not yet. I wasn't able to get ahold of her yet, but now I will make it a priority."

I counted to ten. I supposed this is more personal to me than them, and surely, they had a lot of cases to work on. This was the only one I was worried about.

"Is there anything I should do?" I asked.

"Nothing. Best if you stay out of it and avoid her. I know you said you saw her the other day, but don't go looking."

"Okay, yeah, I wasn't looking for her that day. Just ran into her." Not wholly true, but no point in telling him that.

"Good, but if you do see her, try to go the other way."

"Got it."

I was shaking, mad about it all. What had I done to this woman? Nothing. If she was the daughter of that guy my father killed, I was just as much a victim in it. I was only a child when it happened. How does she think I could have stopped it?

I wonder what happened to her brother. He was just as cheated out of a father and must be just as upset. Did he have memories of his father? He was younger than me by a few years. I tried to think of my earliest memories. How old was I? Maybe three.

Arlo and Noah came outside with the pressure washer. I stepped out of the way as Arlo fired it up. I watched as the spray of water slowly erased the words from the side of the building.

Thank goodness it looked like it was going to work. I continued watching for another minute or two, but I was satisfied that it was going to be removed in time for our lunch crowd.

"Let me know if you need me. I'm going to get ready for the day," I said to Arlo and Noah.

I tried to ignore the whispers and the murmurs as I worked. I knew the staff had questions, but honestly, I didn't have answers. We just had to focus on what we could control.

That was something Mr. Jones taught me in culinary school.

"Can you change the weather? No. So only focus on what you can control." Then he had me cut two pounds of onions into a perfect 1/4-inch dice. "See, you can control this. It is an art, a skill. You're the artist."

I focused all my energy into cooking from that day on, and today I put all my frustration into creating my dishes. As each ticket came in, I cooked and plated as if each was a masterpiece in and of itself.

By the time June came in for the evening shift, I was emotionally spent and just wanted to take a nosedive into my pillows, sleeping for two days. Unfortunately, I couldn't do that as I had to work again tomorrow.

"That graffiti today was so disgraceful. Tsk, tsk. Some people have no respect." June scowled as we traded places. She took over my station as I headed out.

"The police have a lead, but who knows if anything will come of it?"

I noticed Eric, one of my runners, was standing nearby, listening. I looked at him and our eyes locked. He smiled quickly, then scurried back to work. Everyone was curious, so I didn't blame him for listening.

"I probably need to do another staff meeting to address all this." I rubbed my temple. "Not today though, I'm beat."

"Yes, go rest, Chef. I got this." June said, as she spread out her knives and adjusted some items on the prep board.

I chuckled to myself. We had a different style, but she was excellent, and the staff were doing well under her leadership.

"Thanks, that's what I'm going to do," I said.

I stopped by the office first to grab my stuff. I nearly ran into Eric who was coming out of it.

"Oh, hi, Chef," he said a little too loudly.

"Hi."

He hurried back to work without a backward look, but I watched him until he turned into the dining room. What the heck?

"Hey, Chef," Jenn said as I stepped in.

"What was Eric doing in here?"

"He was just asking about the schedule. I told him it would be posted like always."

I nodded. That was a little odd, but not completely unusual, I guess. I think I was simply tired and paranoid.

"Any word on the graffiti?" Jenn asked.

"Not yet. Noah and I gave everything to the officers this morning." I grabbed my purse from inside the desk.

"Glad I missed it."

"Yeah, it was a mess. People were standing around. I'm sure there are tons of posts online about it."

"Yeah, actually I saw some before I came in today. Yikes."

"I was afraid of that. I haven't been online yet. Um, can you add staff meeting to the schedule for Wednesday afternoon?"

That was in two days. Perhaps I'd have some answers by then.

"Alrighty, I will get that added."

"Great. Well, I'm heading out. June is in charge for the night. See ya."

"See ya."

Back in my car, I was ready to head home. I blasted my music all the way, singing at the top of my lungs. It was cleansing. My stress was much lower by the time I parked on the side of our townhouse.

I headed straight in and to the shower, the hot water washing all the grease and grit from me. Thirty minutes later, my skin was bright red and stinging, as I stepped out grabbing my towel.

Lulu sat on the bathroom counter waiting for me.

"Are you waiting for me?" I wrapped the towel around myself. "Did you miss me?"

She meowed and paced on the counter. I reached over and scratched her chin.

I heard my friends coming in.

"Honey, we're home!" Sawyer yelled.

"I'm just getting out of the shower, down in a minute," I yelled to them.

Vee came running up the stairs, bursting into my room. She had no boundaries, and I gave up trying to enforce any on her a long time ago. I ran a brush through my wet hair as she plopped onto my bed.

"I am so sorry about the words on your beautiful restaurant. Did it wash off?"

"It did. Thank goodness."

"What did the police say?"

"Not much, but we think it's that girl, Flora."

"Really? Why would she do that?"

"Your guess is as good as mine. I guess she is holding some weird grudge for not hiring her." I slipped on an extra big T-shirt and some old sweatpants. "You know, I saw her artwork the other day. She's good."

"Oh, right. Apparently, she is some local street artist."

"How do you know that?"

I sat on the other end of my bed. I hadn't told them much after the comic bookstore encounter with her. I had been in a bit of shock, and only mentioned that I saw her, and she hated me. Not about the artwork.

"We asked at work if anyone knew her," Vee said.

There was a knock at the door. Sawyer, like me, had boundaries.

"Come in," I said.

"Did she tell you about that Flora chick?"

"Yeah, she just was. Holy moly. So, what else?"

"Not much. She does have a brother, but nobody knew his name. They're close, though, growing up without a dad and a mourning mother," Sawyer said.

"I can relate, except it was only me. My brothers came later." I did a gagging action with my finger. They laughed knowing my dysfunctional relationship with my brothers. "And I guess my father is still alive. So, they are Jackson's children, then?"

"That's what it sounds like, and it could be a motive for why she is coming for you."

"Well, dang, I need to figure out how to prove it, because I have a feeling that she is going to have an alibi and witnesses that she was with them."

"But how are we going to do that?" Vee asked.

"We?" I laughed.

"Of course, we. How are *we* going to do this?"

"I don't know yet but let me sleep on it. I think better when I'm fresh."

"Well, okay, team misfits are going to solve this murder and the mystery."

"Dinner?" Sawyer said.

"I'll cook." I offered.

Despite being exhausted, I didn't mind. Neither of them could cook, or at least not well, so it often fell to me. There were times I didn't mind going out or ordering pizza, but cooking made me happy, especially for the people I love. I got that from Granny Ines.

Hours later, I was lying in bed, staring at my ceiling. I didn't know how I was going to solve this yet and prove that Jackson's children, or at least Flora, were after me. Also, I didn't know if it was connected to Earl's murder because honestly, what had he done to her?

It was something I was determined to find out.

Chapter Fourteen

When my alarm blasted the next morning, I wanted to throw it across the room. My night had been fitful. My dreams filled with shootings, graffiti, and a laughing demon woman with the most haunting eyes.

The only answer I had when I woke was, it might be time for a visit to my dear ole dad in prison. It was something I always dreaded. However, since there was no Internet back when his trial happened and there had been limited things added about the trial over the years since, I needed something more concrete.

In my mind, going to see him was my best way to get facts about what happened. But that was also the problem. Would he actually tell me the truth or his version of it? My father had never lied to me, that I knew of anyway. However, I knew from my own experiences that you can't always trust your memories.

I pushed out of bed, heading for coffee. Sawyer and Vee would already be at work. Vee left me a sticky note on the coffee pot with a motivational quote. She loved to do that for me, and when I could, I left them for her.

Today's was especially motivating.

Attract what you expect.
Reflect what you desire.
Become what you respect.
Mirror what you admire.

It made me smile. Not because it fit my current life exactly, but it was what I wanted to be in my life. Especially the mirror what you admire.

I had worked so hard to get to this point. Many people questioned why it took me so long to make my dream of owning a restaurant real. Some chefs had been able to open theirs much younger than I am now.

Obviously, I couldn't speak to how they did it and I certainly am not one to tell others how to live their lives. For myself, I wanted to ensure I had enough capital, a solid plan, and enough experience to make it successful.

Failure was not an option, so I had to wait until I felt I could be the most successful. Plus, to be honest, until just a few years ago, I didn't believe in myself enough. Now I had the confidence I didn't have when I was still in my twenties. Each day, and each food competition win, brought more belief in myself.

With coffee in hand, I put a couple of slices of bread in the toaster. Simple, easy breakfast for one. I wasn't in the mood to cook something since I would spend most of my day doing that.

I slathered on my own special blackberry jam. It was something I loved to have on hand. I often gave it out as gifts.

I finished my toast and coffee, then went to get dressed.

"Alrighty, Lulu, don't miss me too much." I grabbed my stuff to leave, checking my reflection once more before heading out the door.

In the car on the way to the restaurant, I hoped I wouldn't find any issues and just have a normal day. I had enough on my mind without adding more issues.

The ride over allowed me to think about my father. I hadn't seen him in over a year.

Granny Ines made me go each year on my birthday. Plus, holidays and his birthday, but I didn't go this year at all because I was working on getting the restaurant open. She went without me but took pictures for him. She had taken a bunch of the restaurant and a mockup of the menu.

"He's so proud of you, Mija. He just wants you to be happy and successful."

I didn't reply, simply smiled at her.

Before the restaurant opened, I would always have Sunday dinner with her and my Aunt Rita. Sawyer and Vee almost always went with me. At different times, my aunt, uncle, and cousins would join us.

Granny Ines would make a ton of food and often would send the leftovers home with us. Mostly for Sawyer. She loved him. Some might argue more than me.

"I love your food, Jessie, but your grandmother is the bomb," Sawyer would say.

"Well, I learned from the best."

I pulled into the parking lot at work. Looked around. Everything looked normal. No crowds, no crime tape, no stalkers.

Heading in, nothing was out of place. I breathed a sigh of relief and just hoped I could get through my shift until June came in so I could head home and straight to bed for a long nap.

I also had a plan to talk to my friends about going to see my dad. They hadn't been with me in years. They never visited with my father but just traveled with me for support. Knowing they were at least nearby had always been a tremendous support, and this time it was definitely needed.

The questions I wanted to ask would be emotional in nature and draining for me. It was something I had tried to block and not remember. The images still haunt my dreams. The shouting, the gunfire, the blood, the screams, and the breaking up of my family.

Then the aftermath, with my mother checking out of motherhood and shipping me to my grandmother and aunt. It was not an ideal childhood.

Though living with my favorite aunt and my grandmother had made it better. They both loved me and gave me the emotional support I needed. Plus, Aunt Rita hosted the best dance parties. We were the only two guests, making it such a special evening.

Still, knowing my mother didn't want me had been a hard burden to live with. It is why I rebelled so much in my teens. Though the stories I heard from others, my stunts were boring compared to them.

All my life, I tried to remember but never could quite recall exactly what led to the shooting. I had always been too afraid to hear the truth, and nobody had offered up the details either.

I made my way through the kitchen and into the office. Nothing looked out of place or crazy.

I fired up the computers so I could check the security camera for the overnight footage, a habit I had gotten into since this whole thing started. I rewound to the day before, and then fast forwarded.

As the clock ticked midnight, I saw on the outside camera, a figure walked by and looked like they stopped before moving on. In fast forward mode it was hard to tell who they were or what they were doing.

I backed it up and then set it to regular speed.

"Is that Flora again?" Noah said, coming in and looking over my shoulder.

She flipped off the camera, looking straight up at it, and looked to be shouting curses at it. I just had to laugh.

"Yep. Classic."

"She seems fun."

"I guess she's pissed that the police interviewed her, or I assume they did."

They hadn't given me an update, but given our late night visit, it seemed a logical reason for her to be upset.

"Do you want to review the sales from yesterday?" Noah asked.

"Yes." I was happy to not think about Flora and her grudge against me.

We got right down to business. Things were looking good. We weren't fully in the black yet, but I could pay everyone and take enough salary for myself to live. It would be a while before I could put more into the business itself, but I was close to calling this successful.

With that bit of business done, I went to the kitchen to get ready for the day.

Like most days, it flew by and soon I was turning over with June for the evening. I loved having her here so I could take time off finally.

"Thanks, June. See you tomorrow." I blew her a kiss, something weird we had just started.

"Night, Chef. Muah!" She blew me a kiss.

I skipped out the door to my car, but before I could get into it, a water balloon smashed against my door.

"Hey!" I turned to find Flora standing behind me. "What the heck?"

"You ratted me out!"

"You painted my restaurant!"

"I did you a favor."

"What? You are sick."

"Yeah, that happens when you grow up without a father!"

"I knew it. You are Jackson's daughter."

"His name was Martin Jackson!" she snarled.

"Okay, but you know I know what it is like to grow up without a father, too, so why are you going at me like this?"

"Ha, you had a father for at least five years, plus he is still alive. Mine is gone, and I never got to know him. Only through pictures and stories."

"And I'm so sorry for that, but I was just a small child. What was I supposed to do?"

"Hire me."

"What?"

"I applied for a chef's position, and you didn't hire me."

"You don't have the experience for it. We offered you a runner position and then you could work your way up."

"Bha, that's so demeaning."

"We all have to start somewhere. You don't just start at the top. It took me years and years to get here."

"Whatever." She crossed her arms hard.

I really didn't understand what she wanted from me. This felt like a ridiculous conversation. No experience for the job you want? You don't get it. At least that's how it works in my world.

"So, now what?" I asked her.

"Hire me."

"I don't have any openings currently, but if I need a busser, dishwasher, or even a server, I will call you."

"That sucks. I don't accept."

"Then get kitchen experience somewhere, even fast food, and we can talk again." I wasn't going to be blackmailed for something I didn't do into giving this random person a job.

"Whatever." She turned, starting to walk away. "This isn't over."

"I like the spunk. Put that into learning about working in a kitchen."

She turned, flipping me the middle finger again.

Boy, she really likes that finger. I thought as I turned to get into my car.

I was able to leave after that without issue.

Heading straight home, I replayed the conversation. Honestly, she had some nerve and the more I thought about it, the more pissed I got.

Why should I just hand her a job? Because of something my father did? No, no, she must have experience just like anyone else out there. I wanted to scream.

Once I got home, it was my usual routine of showering and getting into comfy clothes. I was too mad now to nap, so I put that energy into treating my roommates to a nice meal tonight.

My plan was my famous meatloaf with mashed potatoes and green beans. Something simple, but they both enjoyed my take on it, and it was a comforting meal.

My mother used to cook a lot before my father went to prison, and this was something she made all the time. She started cooking again when she remarried and then had my brothers. This was still my favorite meal, despite my distaste for my new family.

I was in the kitchen working when my friends came home.

"Oh, honey, you're cooking us dinner! Meatloaf? Yay!" Sawyer rushed me, grabbing me into a hug.

"Hey, hey, I have a knife."

He sat me down carefully. "Sorry. I just love your meatloaf! I am taking a meatloaf sandwich for lunch tomorrow," he sang out.

"What's the occasion? Stressful day?" Vee asked as she took a seat at the kitchen island.

Vee knew me too well.

"Flora caught me after work. She wants me to hire her simply because my father killed hers. And yes, she is Martin Jackson's daughter."

"Wow. Really?" Vee's eyes bugged out.

"The nerve!" Sawyer crossed his arms and leaned against the counter, grabbing a raw green bean from the bowl. "What did she say?"

I relayed the conversation, starting with the water balloon.

"Some people feel so entitled."

"What the heck?"

"Yeah, and the weird thing is, I was debating going to see my father to ask him what he knew about Jackson's family."

"That's huge. Are you still going to?" Vee asked.

"I think I am. Granny Ines will be happy and maybe I can get some answers about all this. I really want to know about the brother, too."

"We can go with you," Sawyer offered.

"Yes, we will just wait in the parking lot or in the waiting area. Whatever you need," Vee said.

"Yes, just let us know what you decide. We've got your back."

I put the meatloaf in the oven as I thought about what they said.

"Yeah, I'm going to think about it a day or two, but yes, I'll take you up on the offer, if I go through with this."

"Cool. Road trip!" Sawyer said, launching himself forward. "I'm going to change out of my uniform before dinner. Back in a sec."

Vee came over to hug me and then went to change out of her uniform, too. I stood there for a second. They were my "ride or die," my best friends. They always had my back no matter what.

Staring at the stairs that my friends had just taken to their rooms, I thought how lost I would be without them.

Chapter Fifteen

It was Wednesday afternoon, and I was sipping a peach lemonade while I waited for my staff to gather around for our staff meeting. It was just a quick check in with them on things, specifically the graffiti on the wall and our reputation.

Though I still didn't have answers, exactly. I just knew that Flora was behind the painted words. I didn't yet know who had killed Earl or shot at me and Vivian. That was still yet to be decided.

The dark sedan seemed to be a dead end, at least for now. Based on what the police said about only finding sedans with regular plates, all I could think was they must have put on real plates after they shot at us.

On one hand, the temporary plates made them anonymous, in that someone couldn't look at it and memorize a license plate number. But continuing to have the paper plates, when most other cars didn't have them, also made them easy to identify.

As for the missing and returned resumes, nobody outside of the office staff knew about that, so there was no reason to bring it up.

Plus, it was such an oddball thing, what would I even say about it? I still didn't understand a motive behind that prank.

Same with the security cameras. Nobody on the regular staff knew about that and I didn't have any answers about it, so no point in sharing, especially if someone here was responsible for it. That would just tip them off that we knew.

"Everyone here?" I looked around. Except for Ava, who had taken the day off, not related, everyone else looked to be here. "Okay, thanks everyone for joining me today. I just wanted to address some of the things we have had going on."

"Do they know who killed Earl?"

"What about the spray paint?"

"I'm getting a lot of questions from family and friends."

"Are we safe?"

Wow, I wasn't expecting so many questions so quickly. I thought I would have to draw it out of them. It threw off my train of thought for a moment.

"Um, no to Earl's killer. Yes, on the paint. I think we are all safe, but we should do the buddy system. Nobody should go out late without someone else. As for family and friends, just let them know ... well, just say the police are doing the best they can to find the killer."

"So, who was the graphic artist?" Parker asked.

Most of the staff sat forward. I guess there wasn't a reason to withhold the information. Word would likely get out soon enough. I wanted to build trust with my team, so I would just tell them what I know.

"She is a local artist named Flora. She had applied for a job here several months ago, as a line cook, but didn't have enough experience for that. I offered her a non-cooking position and she declined. Since then, she is holding a grudge."

"That doesn't sound related to Earl," Stelly mumbled.

"Yeah, I think we're good," Marco added.

Though I had to wonder what he would be worried about. He was built like a barn and had come in quite handy when that one interview went south.

"Any other questions or concerns?"

Nobody really had any other questions, so we went through broiler plate stuff, like soup of the day, the daily specials, and upcoming days off and schedules.

"Schedules will be up for next week later today," Noah said. "We have a few folks taking days off, so things might be a touch different the next few weeks with the schedule, so be sure to check it."

We ended the meeting after that. People mingled a bit. I finished my lemonade and then hopped off the bar stool to return to the kitchen, but on my way, I ran right into Eric.

"Whoops, sorry about that. I didn't see you." I chuckled.

"It's okay," He mumbled, but didn't move on, just kept staring at me.

"Did you have a question?" I asked him.

"No, nothing," he said, barely audible.

"Um, okay. Well, take care." I started to walk away.

He mumbled something, then stomped off in the other direction.

What the bleep? I thought.

He was a strange person, but he had limited interactions with the customers, so I didn't mind.

It was nearly the end of his shift. Perhaps he was just a bit grumpy and tired. I could understand that. I was pretty tired myself.

I looked over at Noah, who just shrugged at me. Since Noah seemed unconcerned by the weird behavior, I took it as a sign to just shrug it off too. He had more direct contact with the staff in the dining room than I did, so I would trust him.

Heading into the kitchen, I went straight to touch base with June. She would be in charge for the evening, and I was going to head home, take a long bath with a glass of wine, then sleep until morning.

At least that was the plan, we would see if that was actually how my night went. Lately, my evenings seemed to go off the rail a bit.

"Your pimento cheese has been a good addition, and everyone is requesting it."

"I know. I have been making double batches each night now, just so we will have enough for the day."

"Any questions before I go home?"

"Nope, nothing."

"Great." I knew when we hired her, it was going to be a smooth transition. I had peace of mind each time I left it in her very capable hands.

I headed to the office where Noah was packing up to head home. Jenn was typing on the computer.

"I think the staff meeting was good." I said.

"Yeah, nothing super surprising." Noah commented.

"Short and sweet," Jenn added.

"I just wish we would hear something from the police. It has been a few days since I've heard anything at all from them, and that wasn't much."

"Wanna walk out with me?" Noah asked.

"Yeah, let me just grab my purse." As I picked it up out of the drawer, it felt weird. I opened it. "What the bleep?"

"What's wrong?"

"It looks like someone went through my purse."

"What?" Noah and Jenn came to look over my shoulder.

"It doesn't seem like anything is missing," I said as I thumbed through it. Everything looked in place. "Yeah, it all seems here, but why did it feel so heavy?"

That's when I noticed there was a heavy envelope at the bottom. I pulled it up and looked at it. My immediate thought was to call the detective to report this.

"I shouldn't open this, right?"

"I wouldn't. I would call Detective Upton and let the police open it." Noah said. He was usually the voice of reason, and I knew he was right.

I nodded and dialed the detective's number. When he answered, I let him know what I'd found.

"I have no idea how it got here or when?"

"I'll be right over with a team. Don't touch anything else. Just leave it as is."

"Okay, thanks, Detective," I hung up. "Okay, he is on his way. I'll go let the front staff know so that they can send him back when he gets here."

My feet felt heavy as I made my way to the front of the restaurant. What the heck was happening in my life? Before opening this restaurant, I lived a fairly predictable life. Nothing crazy really happened, at least not since I became an adult and started to steer my own life.

"Hey, y'all, just to let you know, Detective Upton is on his way. Please send him back to the office when he gets here."

Tyler and Jordan exchanged a look but agreed without questioning me. After our staff meeting, I am sure they were hopeful that this was about Earl. I wish it was.

I walked through the dining room, greeting customers.

"Mom?" My mouth fell open when I saw my mother, stepfather, and both of my brothers sitting there with pimento cheese and our crawfish stuffed mushrooms. "What are y'all doing here?"

They had yet to come eat at the restaurant. We didn't have the best relationship and outside of holidays, we rarely talked or saw each other. I mean, I had updated her on things with the restaurant, but it was via text.

"We're here for a late lunch, or I guess early dinner." She grinned. "This cheese is amazing!"

"We're very proud of you, Jessie," Samuel said with a grin. I wanted to barf. He was so fake sometimes.

"Thanks."

I tried to sound cheerful, but in the back of my mind, I wanted them gone before the officers got here. Considering they were only on the appetizers, it seemed likely they'd be here still.

This is not what I need right now.

Christopher and Bryan were playing on their phones and never looked up. I tried to come up with something to say, but my brain was frozen.

"So, what did you order?" It was an awkward attempt to connect.

"Oh, well, I got the chicken and dumplings, Sam got the chicken fried steak, and the boys got burgers."

"Okay, nice. I hope you enjoy it."

At that moment, the officers walked in. Chris and Bryan's heads snapped up. They smirked at each other.

"Someone's in trouble." Bryan snickered.

"What did you do now, Messy-Jessie?" Christopher laughed. That was a nickname they came up with when they were young. I hated it.

"Nothing. It's just business stuff." I flashed a fake smile. "Please excuse me. I hope you enjoy your meal."

I walked away, trying not to hear what my family said behind my back. My mom and Samuel started arguing and pointing fingers at my father's influence. I mentally shook off their words so I could focus on the issue at hand.

"Hi, Detective, officers." I smiled at them, trying to remain professional and calm, even though I could still hear my brothers' mocking comments behind me. "Follow me to the office."

All eyes, from customers to staff, followed us as we walked to the back of the house. Most people knew about Earl and the graffiti, so hopefully that was what they thought this was about. Still, it was nerve-racking. All I wanted was to share my love of cooking with people.

"Here is what I found." I handed him the envelope, but he didn't take it right away. First, he slipped on some latex gloves.

"Just in case."

A hot wave of realization came over me at the thought that I could have been exposed to something. I guess I knew that there was a danger of a poison or drug of some sort being in it, or why else would I have called him? But I'd only thought of if I opened it, not something being on the outside of it.

"Should I be worried? I've touched it and it's been in my purse."

"No, it should be fine but just want to follow procedures."

Detective Upton sounded sincere, and I wanted to trust him. But I was going to be washing my hands many, many times after they left, and probably throw out my purse.

He opened the envelope and pulled out a stack of papers. He flipped through them, but I couldn't quite see what was on the pages.

"These look like resumes." He turned them towards me then.

"Oh, what?"

I grabbed some gloves from one of the officers, then took the resumes from him. I couldn't believe what I was seeing.

"These are current employees."

Someone had written notes, all of them like liar, slut, and slacker. It was weird.

"Why would someone do this?" Noah said, reading over my shoulder.

We looked at each other. This finally pushed me out of my denial. I liked to think of it more as wishful thinking. This was not someone outside of the restaurant who had done this. It was, most definitely, one of my staff members doing this.

Now the question was who?

"We can take this down to the station and see if we can run it through our database, find a handwriting match or try to pull prints. Just see if we can figure this out." Detective Upton said, nodding to the officer with him.

He whipped out a plastic bag, slipped the resumes into it, including the envelope, and then sealed it. Next, he scribbled something on a label and attached that to the bag.

"We should check the security footage, too."

Jenn tapped into the computer, pulling up the camera recordings.

"Where do you want to start?"

"Well, my purse has been here since 9 this morning, so I guess start there."

I could feel Noah staring at me. I didn't mean to imply he had anything to do with it, but that from the time my purse went into that desk drawer until a few minutes after 3, anyone could have come in here.

"Okay, here we go." She set the speed to a fast, but reviewable speed.

We watched Noah and I talking, I left while he turned to work on the computer. Then after some time, he left and returned, left and returned. Jordan came in to call him away. I assume a customer needed him.

Then the office was empty for about an hour. Checking the time it was right in the middle of the lunch rush. Nothing really exciting happened until the three of us came back after the staff meeting when I found the envelope in my purse.

Nothing. How could that be?

"Nothing." Noah exhaled.

"Can we get a copy of that?" Detective Upton said, pulling out his ever available USB drive, handing it to Jenn.

"Coming up." She clicked a few things, waited, then handed it to the detective.

"Thanks. We'll call you if we need any additional information," Detective Upton said.

"Or, if you find something, right?"

His hesitation told me all I needed to know. He would not give me more than he thought necessary. I could only assume this was an order from Chief Stone.

"Of course, I will." He smiled.

"Oh, and I assume you interviewed Flora?"

"Yeah, we did. She didn't deny it. We issued a citation, and she has a court date. Why do you ask?"

I kept my first thought to myself, which was, why didn't he tell me? Why had it taken me asking for him to tell me about her?

"We saw her on the overnight footage flipping off our camera. Nothing was wrong. I guess she just wanted to let me know her distaste at the charge."

"Ah, but no other problems?"

"Well, except for the resumes, no. She couldn't have done that without help from an employee."

"Anyone you can think of?"

"Not a soul. I trust all my employees."

Even though I'd moved out of denial, I didn't have a name to give, so I couldn't point the finger at all of them.

"Alright. Well, I think we have everything, but if you have any other trouble, give me a call."

"We will. I'll walk you out."

I walked them out and was relieved to see that my family had left. I would have to ask Jordan, who was the current host, how long ago and if they said anything.

At least they weren't here to see me walking out the officers.

"Well, thank you for coming out. I look forward to hearing any news about this or Earl's death."

"Of course," he said, before they all went out the front door.

I stared at the closed door for only a moment. Turning towards the host stand, I smiled at Jordan.

"How long ago did my family leave?"

"Oh, just a minute or two."

"Did they say anything?"

"Not really. They just said thanks and walked out."

I let out a huge sigh of relief. Though I wasn't going to share with my employees about my dysfunctional, crazy family, but glad to hear they hadn't made a scene.

"Thanks." I smiled then returned to the office.

Noah and Jenn were talking, and went silent when I came in.

"Uh-oh, am I the weird kid?" I laughed.

"No, nothing like that. Just talking about inventory. Nothing special," Noah said.

"And Parker took the next couple of days off." Jenn frowned.

"Yeah, that's okay. He has been working hard," I said.

"Yeah, but the rumor is, he's looking for another job," Jenn said.

"Oh, well, I guess he has that right." I didn't like to hear that, but he had the right to do that if he wanted. Though if I were honest with myself, I have spent hours training him to be a sous chef. If he took that experience elsewhere, that would hurt deeply.

"You walking out?" Noah asked.

"Yeah, you ready too?"

"Yep, take care, Jenn."

"See you tomorrow."

"Night, y'all," she said, smiling.

When we were in the parking lot, he looked around, then turned to me.

"I think it's Jenn." He whispered so quietly that I almost didn't hear him.

"I'm sorry?"

"I don't know why I think that, but I was looking at her face when the detective was there. She just had this look of guilt, or I don't know, something, it was a slight smirky smile."

"But, why? Why would she do that?"

"This is someone on the inside doing all this stuff, right? She has access. Nobody is there at night to watch her while she works, and she is the one who hired the security company. Could she be the one editing the footage?" He tapped his temple.

"But why would she do that?"

"That I don't know, yet. Just trust me."

His eyes told me he was sincere, but why should I trust him? He was pointing a finger at her. Could it be a tactic to throw me off?

For some reason though, I decided to believe him. I needed to trust someone and the sincerity in his eyes told me a lot.

"What do you think about Parker? Do you think he is looking for another job?" I asked. Could all of this be Parker?

"No, that is just people spreading stuff, and you see it was Jenn who put that in your head."

"True." I nodded.

"Seriously, don't give that another thought. I know Parker and he wouldn't do that. He is thankful for you taking him under your wing."

"Okay. I trust you." Or, at least, I really wanted to.

"Thank you."

I scanned the parking lot. The idea of looking over my shoulder or side-eying all my employees didn't sit well with me. I wanted to build a team of trust, loyalty, and a positive work environment. We weren't off to a good start with a murder and then all this weirdness.

"Have a good night."

"Night, Chef." He smiled and went to his car, driving away immediately.

I hesitated to drive away as I took a long look at the restaurant. This was my dream, and I wasn't going to give up without a fight.

As I put it in reverse to back up, there was a loud thump sounding like it came from the rear of my car.

Bleep! I hadn't even moved yet.

I looked in all the mirrors but didn't see anything, so I put it back in park, then got out to check things out. Walking all around my car, I didn't see anything. Not a person. Not an animal.

What the heck? I thought.

That's when I saw Eric standing at the other side of the parking lot. Did he do it?

"Hey, Eric. Did you see anything hit my car?"

"Nope."

I hesitated a moment, trying to gage his body language. Nothing seemed to unusual.

"Huh. Okay. Thanks."

I guess I was dreaming it, but I kept an eye on him while I left the parking lot. Driving home, I watched in my rearview to see if anyone followed me. I'd never been followed, so I wasn't sure what to look for. Paranoid was the only way to describe my state of mind as I pulled up at home.

Safe.

Chapter Sixteen

I looked at the clock. *Darn it.* Time to get up but I hadn't slept well all night as my mind had been replaying the conversation with Noah from yesterday.

Jenn had a lot of responsibilities, being she was the assistant manager. She had access to the safe, the accounts, our security cameras, and many other things.

If she had tampered with the resumes and security footage, that would be such a betrayal of trust. She came with good references and years of experience.

Plus, it would be a blow to my confidence with future hires and it would hurt our business a lot.

I was going to have to wade carefully as I investigated her. If she wasn't guilty, it could really hurt our relationship, but not knowing would hurt it too. So, this was a lose-lose.

Then Parker, gosh, I hope it was just a rumor. He had come a long way in the past few weeks with his training. I was close to letting him take the day shift by himself. If he left, I would have to start over with a new line cook to train up to an assistant sous chef role.

Hannah and Stelly were my next two, but they were going to take several months to get to where Parker is now. I had faith they could get there, too.

Having them all trained would allow me to step back even further and be more of an owner than a chef or even allow me to work on another project. Perhaps catering or a food truck.

If that wasn't enough to keep me up at night, today I was off as I was going to see my father. My nerves were working overtime as I thought about seeing him. I hated the fakeness of our visits.

He wanted to act like life was normal, as he asked me about my life, was I dating, how was school or now work, and give me fatherly advice. Yet here he was, sitting in prison for murder. Why would I listen to him? Things weren't normal.

I hated my childhood, and I hated him for robbing me of that.

But I just wanted to know what he knew about the Jacksons, if anything.

I stretched, which disturbed Lulu, who had been sleeping at the foot of my bed. She shot me a dirty look before jumping from the bed.

"Sorry, Lulu."

Being a cat, she didn't reply but continued out of my room. She was probably going to see if she could get into Sawyer's room. He kept it dark, and she liked that.

I headed first to the bathroom and then straight for the coffee pot.

"Good morning," Vee said as she helped herself to a mug full and then added her flavored creamer. "Are you ready for today?"

"Morning. No, I'm never ready for this." I grabbed a mug, then filled it. The bitter, almost nutty aroma hit me. The scent alone was almost enough to wake me up.

We sat together at the kitchen island area. This was my favorite part of the townhouse. It was a five-foot-long island with a bar area on one side. Even though we had a breakfast table, we sometimes ate our meals here, especially quicker things or when it was just one or two of us eating.

"Well, just get in there, talk to him, and then get out. After we'll go for drinks after."

"I'd rather hit Rosie's for a giant milkshake and a burger." I chuckled.

Rosie's Diner was our favorite place since we were kids. We often went to celebrate or to eat away stress. When everyone else was at prom, the three of us went to Rosie's for dinner and then out to Vee's family lake house. We had a bonfire and some cheap beers that Vee's mom bought us. It was a perfect night.

"We can do that."

Sawyer came in yawning. He got his coffee and joined us.

"Late night?" Vee teased.

"Yeah, bad date. Bad, *bad* date."

Vee and I exchanged a look. Sawyer always said that. He had high standards for women, and they never lived up to it.

"Oh, no. What happened?" I asked mockingly.

He stared at me for a second. "I know you're teasing, but seriously, she was the worst. I couldn't get her to talk much at all. When she did talk, it was a mumble."

"The horror." Vee laughed.

"She has some nerve," I added.

"Y'all are the worst. But you know when you are trying to get to know someone, you hope they will engage in conversation with you."

"Yeah, that is actually not fun," I agreed. "We just tease you because we love you."

"I don't even know why I asked her out, but she seemed cool online." He shook his head.

"They always are." Vee said.

We sighed in unison. We all had our fair share of bad dates, especially from online apps. It almost had me ready to throw in the towel on finding my person and just be happily single with my cat.

"So, what time are we leaving today?" he asked.

"Nine?" I asked.

"Alright. Are you nervous?"

"Rosie's Diner nervous," Vee said for me.

"Ah, got it. Double cheeseburger and an extra chocolaty, chocolate shake nervous." He nodded.

"I'll make us some omelets," I said, taking a large gulp of coffee. Cooking would settle my nerves, or at least for a few minutes.

An hour later, we were loading into Sawyer's car and heading to the Milton County Prison. It was a roughly two-hour drive or two and a half if I was going with Granny Ines.

My friends tried to distract me from my own thoughts. I mostly stayed quiet on the trip. I had to get in the right mindset to see him.

We pulled into the visitor parking lot, and the butterflies in my stomach turned into a swarm of bees. Steadying my breathing, I climbed out of the car.

"Do you want us to stay here or come with you to the waiting area?" Sawyer said, leaning over the top of his car.

"Can you just walk me in? I'm afraid I'm going to run."

"Sure."

They both followed me up to the door and waited while I got checked in. They would wait in the waiting room while I visited with my father.

I signed in, showed my driver's license, then went through the metal detector. The officer stationed at the door to let people into the visiting room was a familiar face.

"Hiya, Ms. Jessica." Officer Luna Pena smiled. "Haven't seen you here in a while."

"Hi, Luna. Yeah, it's been a bit."

"Your grandmother said you opened your restaurant. That's wonderful."

"Thanks. Yes, we've been open about two months now."

"Oh, fantastic. I'll have to drive to Dashwood for a visit. My mom is still there, you know?"

"Nice. We'd love to have you visit us."

She waved me into the room. I walked to the table that was reserved for our visit and then waited for my dad. I looked around at the concrete gray cinder block walls. They were lined with framed prints of various landscapes. I guess to give the illusion of the outside world, but I mostly got cheap motel room vibes from them.

I glanced at the other tables of families and friends waiting. This part never got easier to see. Crying babies, young children whining, and sullen teenagers just ready to leave. I was all of those at one time, except the baby. I had a father until I was in kindergarten.

A bell chimed, signaling that the inmates were on the way. People around straightened to prepare for their loved one coming through the door. There was an excitement in the air, but unlike many of them, I was bracing myself.

"Jessie!" My dad burst forward from the line. He quickly hugged me.

A corrections officer cleared his throat. I smiled nervously at Officer Chuck Martindale. He had been a regular here since I was a teen.

As my father backed up, I took him in fully. He had aged gracefully. Almost no gray hair, just enough to give him a distinguished look. Crow's feet around his eyes, which looked more like laugh lines from years of laughter versus a life behind bars. He was still fit and had gotten a few prison tattoos, but otherwise, he looked like my father.

"Sorry, Chuck," Dad said. "I just haven't seen my girl in over a year."

"I get it, Tito, just watch it." Officer Martindale said.

"It's so good to see you, Mija. How are you? How is the restaurant?" He gestured for us to sit.

"Everything is going well. The restaurant has been packed. We have rave reviews."

"I read some of them online. I'm so proud of you."

"Thanks. How are you?"

"Can't complain too much. I have a new cellmate. Guy is struggling a lot, but I hope to get him through the rough days." He continued telling me about this friend or that. There was some big fight, and he helped to deescalate it. "The anger management classes in here have helped a lot." He laughed.

It was the same deep laugh I remember as a child, but in this room, it echoed in a mocking way that sent a chill through my body. I really hated it here.

"So, I know this isn't a friendly visit, Mija. You have fought for a while not to come anymore. Does this have anything to do with the death of your sous chef?"

I shouldn't be surprised that he knew. He had access to the Internet, though they limited what they could see. He had always kept up with news from home.

"Actually, no, well, it might be related, but I'm not sure."

"Well, what is it?"

"There is this woman that seems to have it out for me. She applied for a job as a chef, but wasn't qualified, so I didn't hire her. Since then, she has done random things, like painting vulgar words on my building and tried to pick up the victim's paycheck from me. She has made a scene, yelling at me about how I owe her because you killed her father."

Though I tried to stay calm, my voice rose. Chuck cleared his throat. I flashed him a sheepish smile and mouthed that I was sorry.

My dad rubbed his chin.

"And what do you need from me?"

"I wanted to know what you know about Mr. Jackson's family, especially his children."

"Oh, Jessie, I don't know much. They had a son named Alistair, and his wife was pregnant with a girl. She was born not long after … well, you know. I think her name was Florence or Fiona? Something with an F.”

“Flora?”

“Yes, that’s it. Flora,” he confirmed.

“That’s the girl, er, woman that is messing with me.”

“I’m not sure what I can do to help.”

I sighed. I wasn’t sure either, but it was worth a try.

“I guess, I didn’t know if you had any information on them. How did you know him? Were you friends? Have you heard anything from them over the years? She seems so angry, so I wasn’t sure if maybe she would have tried to say something to you.”

“No, nothing. I didn’t know him very well. He worked for me at the machine shop. We sometimes hosted cookouts for the employees. He came a few times. Sometimes with his family, sometimes alone.”

I had a vague memory of having parties at our house. I guess I didn’t remember the details about who the people were. That explained how we knew them.

As I thought about my next question, I noticed a shadow cross over his normally jovial face.

“What aren’t you telling me?”

He looked over at Chuck, then leaned forward. “I have received a few threats over the years, but lately they are every week. I’m not sure how the letters made it to me, because they typically screen everything.”

That was alarming. Was someone in here also working to sabotage me? Was it a guard or a prisoner? My mind was spinning. While I was mad at my father for his choice, I didn’t want him to be in danger.

“Are you safe?” I lowered my voice to ask.

His eyes darted around. “Yeah, I think so. I mean, I’m pretty tough.” He flexed his arms and pectoral muscles. I had to admit, he was quite fit for a sixty-year-old man. “Plus, being that I murdered someone, I get threats a lot. This isn’t really that new.”

I chuckled softly. That’s the father I remembered. Well, the joking one. I hated to hear he received threats a lot.

“Aw, I missed your laugh, Jessie.” He reached for my hand but withdrew it. We couldn’t touch again until the end of the visit.

"Please, you be safe out there. I made an enemy, and it seems they are looking to even things."

His words sent an icy chill down my spine. I simply nodded because I didn't trust myself to speak.

The bell sounded, signaling the visit was over. At the sound, tears sprung to my eyes. I couldn't explain the emotion because as much as I dreaded seeing him, having to leave him felt just like the night he was arrested and being ripped from me forever.

We quickly hugged and said goodbye. I watched as he lined up and walked out, joking with a couple of the other men. As the door closed, I saw him turn to look at me. He mouthed "I love you" as the door slammed between us.

Visitors started to exit. I stood back so that I would be the last to leave. I'm not sure why, but something in me just didn't want to leave my father. It was this mix of emotions that made each visit so difficult. It was the dread then the loss all over again. I hated it.

"How did it go?" Vee popped up when I came into the lobby.

"I'll tell you on the drive home," I said, my voice catching in my throat.

They wrapped their arms around me as we left. It was going to be a tearful ride home, but at least I had Rosie's Diner to look forward to on the way back.

Chapter Seventeen

The double cheeseburger and extra chocolate milkshake at Rosie's Diner helped my weary soul. The visit with my dad was fine, actually better than I expected. However, hearing that he had received threats worried me.

It made me concerned for him. He couldn't hide or run from an attacker. Though I had to have faith, he could handle himself. He was a tough guy. Over the years, he had several fights and once, for my birthday, our visit to see him had been canceled because of a brawl he started.

At eight years old, it was hard to understand. Heck, at thirty-five, it wasn't much easier to understand.

As I was settling in for the night, my phone sent an alert. It was my security alarm.

That's strange. The crew should have closed up and gone home already. I thought.

I pulled up the app that allowed me to look at the security cameras. Nothing looked obvious on the camera, but I probably should go check it out given the recent issues.

As I was looking for clothes, the alarm company called.

"Hello. This is Miller Alarms. We had an alarm, but it has reset on its own. Do you want us to send the police?"

"No, I'm going to check it out. I'm sure my staff didn't set the system correctly or something wasn't secured properly. They just left thirty or so minutes ago."

"Okay. Please call us if you need any help."

I thanked them and then pulled on an extra-large bleach-stained sweatshirt over my sleep shirt and then pulled on baggy sweats. I completed my wonderful outfit with bear paw slippers. It was a look. Maybe it would scare off burglars. I laughed quietly at the thought.

Once I was dressed, I went to see if Sawyer was still awake. I found him playing video games in the living room.

"Hey, can you go with me to the restaurant? The alarm was going off and I just need to check it."

"Yeah, just let me …. Oh! Boom, baby." He dropped his controller and began a crazy victory dance. "That's what I'm talking about."

"I have no idea." I laughed.

My phone sent me another notification about the alarm. "Dang it."

My phone rang again, and I once again I assured them I was heading over to check it. I would call the police if anything looked strange.

"Wow, maybe we should call the police to meet us there?" Sawyer said, as he slipped into his well-worn tennis shoes.

They had duct tape keeping them together, and he'd drawn all over them with a marker. He called these his house shoes, but on occasion, he wore them outside of the house, just like my bear paw slippers.

"Let's just drive over and see if there is anything we can see. If it looks crazy, we'll call them."

At that moment, Vee came downstairs.

"Oh, hey, didn't know you were still awake?" I said.

"I was reading and heard voices. What's going on?"

"The alarm at the restaurant keeps going off." As if on cue, it did it again and again I talked to the alarm company. This was annoying.

"I wanna go." She ran to grab flip-flops and a sweater.

I'm sure if a burglar was there, we would be a scary sight. Me with bleach stains, Sawyer with his duct taped shoes, and Vee with her cute elf like look. Okay, perhaps she was more cute than scary.

With Sawyer as the driver, we headed over. At nearly one in the morning, the streets were empty except for a few cats and a stray dog. We pulled up to the front of the restaurant.

"Nothing looks out of place here," I said, looking around.

"I don't see any lights," Vee said, peering out the back window.

Sawyer eased the car slowly down from the front, around to the side facing the street, and then around to the side parking near the back door.

There weren't any cars or shadows of people standing nearby hiding. The back door looked closed, and the floodlights were on casting the entire lot in light, making it hard for someone to hide.

"This is weird."

"Should we go check out inside?" Sawyer offered.

"Yeah, I better."

He parked near the back door, and we all climbed out. I unlocked the door, and we scrambled in so I could shut off the alarm upon entering. I turned on the light.

We walked through the kitchen into the office checking each camera from the ground. I especially wanted to look at the sensor facing the dishwashing area. This is where the alarm kept triggering.

"Do you think it was a bug or something?" Sawyer asked.

"Ew, no. I just got a health inspection done, and I didn't have any bugs. I keep things clean. Plus, that's so bad for business." But I looked closer at the camera that was causing the alarm, just in case.

From the ground, I couldn't see anything.

With the back secure, I went out to the dining area and bar, just to check. Nothing looked out of place. This was puzzling.

"Everything looks secure and how it should after we close," I said, looking around once more.

"So, what? We just lock up and head home?" Sawyer asked.

"I guess so. It must have been a fluke."

We backtracked through the kitchen. I checked around once more before I set the alarm, and we piled back into the car. We sat for a minute as I confirmed on the security app that everything looked good.

"Alright, I guess we head home."

Sawyer nodded and put it in gear; however, before we could pull out of the parking lot, a car came speeding around the corner. It stopped facing us, and flashed its brights.

"What do we do?" Vee gasped from the backseat.

Before we could decide, the car backed up, then sped forward, straight for us. A blood-curdling scream came from the back seat. Thankfully the car turned just before hitting us. A single hand came from the driver's seat, or should I say, one finger.

"Freaking Flora." I grumbled as my heart started to beat again.

"You think that was her?" Sawyer asked.

"Yeah, I would recognize that finger anywhere."

"Why would she do that? What is she even doing out here?"

"She probably saw us here and took a chance. Not sure about the late hour. At least she didn't shoot at us or anything."

"I think I nearly wet myself," Vee said.

"TMI, girl." I laughed.

Sawyer chuckled and finally pulled out of the parking lot. We arrived home without further incident, but that trip really cut into my sleep for the night. I already knew I was going to struggle to fall asleep with everything on my mind, but now it was an hour and a half closer to my morning wake up.

"You gonna be okay?" Vee asked, wrapping her arms around me when we got inside.

"Yeah, are you?"

"I don't know. That was scary."

"It was exciting!" Sawyer chuckled. "Got my blood pumping. I'm ready to face off with more zombies."

His long legs took him to the couch, where he began playing another round of his game.

"Well, I have to be up by 8 am, so I'm going to call it," I said. "I just hope that the alarm is good for the night."

I climbed the stairs, stripped out of my extra clothes, and belly flopped onto my bed. Next thing I remember, my alarm was going off, telling me it was time to get up.

Whoa, I don't even remember falling asleep, I thought as I stretched.

I went about my morning routine and then headed downstairs for coffee and a quick breakfast. Lulu happily jogged down the stairs with me. She had been clingy since I started working more.

"Hey, what are you doing awake?"

"Oh, dang, is it morning already?" He rubbed his eyes. "I guess I pulled an all-nighter. Want me to make us some coffee?"

"I got it." I laughed.

He had quite a cozy life, and I was glad to be part of it for roughly twenty-five years. I walked over to the couch, kissing his check.

"What was that for?"

"Just thinking about how grateful I am for you."

"Don't get mushy on me, or you might just fall in love with me." He winked.

"Hey, if I haven't yet, I'm probably safe."

We both laughed. It had never crossed our minds to date. We simply didn't have that type of relationship.

"Well, I guess I'm going to sleep," he said, shutting off his game.

I watched him as he made his way up the stairs. After my coffee was ready, I took it to the kitchen island and then checked my phone. I scrolled through social media, checked my emails, and then viewed the security cameras to see if everything was okay at the restaurant.

Nothing. That's good.

I stared at the bottom of my coffee mug. Half of me wanted another cup, but the other half knew if I didn't go get ready now, I would be late. I needed time to talk with Noah about what he'd told me the other day about Jenn and touch base about the security alarm.

Sighing, I rinsed out my mug and stuck it in the dishwasher before going to get ready for work. I dressed in my chef clothes, then headed to my favorite place in the world.

Arriving, I took an extra hard look around. Only Arlo's car was visible. I could see he was out front, power washing the sidewalks. I liked to keep things neat and tidy. Lucky for me, Arlo did too. He was the best maintenance guy I could have hired.

"Mornin', Arlo," I yelled at him.

He simply waved and then focused on the sidewalk. Thankfully, it was just normal cleaning, and not due to graffiti.

I walked into the stainless-steel kitchen that I owned. Each time I walked into it, I was in awe of the beauty. I breathed in a deep cleansing breath, soaking it all in. I did this nearly every morning. Even after two months open, I couldn't believe this was mine. I could pinch myself every morning.

I flipped on the rest of the lights that Arlo hadn't already. Then I began my normal prep for the day while I waited for Noah.

By the time employees started to show up, I had already prepped my entire station, plus got the soups started for the day.

"Soup of the day, Tomato and Basil," I yelled out as the line cooks and servers arrived. They all nodded.

"Good morning, Jess," Noah said, when he arrived. "Ready to chat?"

"Yep. Let me wash my hands and I'll meet you in the office."

"No, can we meet in my car?"

I stared at him for a moment. His car? That was an odd request. I guess, sensing my hesitation, he stepped closer.

"Just in case the office is bugged or something. I swear, nothing weird," He whispered.

"Oh, yeah, that makes sense. I'll be right there."

I went to wash my hands and as I turned to throw my paper towel away, I saw Eric watching me.

"Oh, good morning, Eric."

"Chef." He mumbled and then turned to ready his cart for cleanup.

Okay. He wasn't the friendliest guy, I thought as I walked out the door.

Looking around the parking lot, I found Noah was standing against his car, flipping through his phone.

"Hey, alright, whatcha got for me?" I asked.

He gestured for me to get in as he opened the driver's side door to get in himself.

"Okay, so I talked to a buddy of mine." He paused, studying me for a second. "Actually, I think you guys would hit it off if you're ever interested."

"Um, interested in dating?"

"Yeah, good guy. Knows computers, which is why I talked to him. He does cybersecurity or something. Honestly, I don't understand it."

"You think I would hit it off with him because he likes computers?" I barely liked computers. Why would I be interested in someone because they liked computers? It seemed so random.

"No, no. He … just he is a nice guy, and I think you both have the same sense of humor. He loves food. Never mind, that's not the point." He rubbed his hand over his face. "I asked him about our security footage, and he found that this company and equipment can be easily tampered with. Which led me to thinking, Jenn is the one that recommended this program, right? She worked with the vendor to set it up. She holds all the passwords.”

“Not all. I have the primary one.”

“Maybe. Or maybe she just told you that.”

“But why would she do that?”

“I don’t know. That’s what we need to figure out.”

“I just can’t think of a reason why. I pay her well. She has a great schedule; one she picked out.”

“Exactly, she picked the evening shift. What better time to do bad things?”

I stared at him. I can’t believe what he was saying.

“No, I really don’t think it’s her. Why would she do this? What does she have to gain from this?”

“That I don’t know yet, but I keep finding weird things in the books too.” He pulled out his phone. He showed me a screenshot on his phone. “See this one here? I don’t know this vendor.”

I looked and didn’t recognize the vendor either. It wasn’t a lot of money, just about sixty dollars. Most of our vendors were food and we spent thousands a month, so this was random.

“How many of these payments are there?”

“Just two about three weeks apart.”

“Did you look up the vendor? Like on the internet?”

“Yeah, looks like a dry cleaner. Maybe for our towels and napkins? But we send those to that place on West Street.”

I don’t know why this didn’t alarm me much. We would just ask her who the vendor was. Perhaps she couldn’t get our things into the regular place.

“So, we’ll both keep our eye on her, and we can ask her about this vendor. Okay?”

Not sure why I suggested asking her. I sucked at confrontation, especially if I thought it might hurt the other person’s feelings. Not exactly good qualities of a boss. I’d have to figure out the best way to ask her about it.

“Okay. Fair enough.”

We talked a few minutes more before going back inside and got on with our day. I had no idea what or how I would figure out what to do with Jenn. She had become someone I thought I could trust, but Noah had a point.

He kept saying the same things and it was starting to make sense to me.

If the footage was being edited, it could be her. She knew the system better than we did. She was the closing person, so she could easily do it once both Noah and I were gone for the day.

Even on the days I was there in the evening, I was busy in the kitchen, so it wasn't like I could watch her the entire time. She moved back and forth between the office and the dining area as she managed the restaurant in the evening. Noah did it during the day.

I just couldn't figure out a motive. What did she have to gain from this? Why would she do it? I couldn't answer either of those questions.

I was going to have to watch for warning signs, I supposed, but what? It was definitely going to keep me up at night until I resolved this.

Chapter Eighteen

Sunday, I had the entire day off, so my friends and I were going to the local art festival. Dashwood had a huge art scene. Everything from folk art to realism to street art. There would be performing arts on two stages that were set up in the town park.

I had thought about having a booth, but it would have meant committing months ago, and with the restaurant launching, I just didn't have time.

Maybe next time, I told myself. This one was a quarterly event, so I had four chances each year.

I dressed in my favorite Neal Barney t-shirt. Neal Barney was a local artist who took mythical creatures and made them in a folklore style of art. His canvas of choice was clothing.

I had several of his tees, but this one with the folk art witch was my favorite. She had on a black dress and was framed with ruby red roses and thorny whimsical vines. She was posed with one finger pressed to her lips as if asking you to keep her secret. It was an amazing piece.

I hoped he was at the festival today, so I could get a new one. Not that I needed more. I had about five of his shirts. Perhaps I could get a messenger bag with a print on it. I had my eye on those at the last festival. It could replace my current ratty hobo bag.

I made my way downstairs to find Sawyer was also wearing a Neal Barney shirt. Thankfully, he was wearing a completely different design. His shirt had a bigfoot trimmed with folksy maple and oak leaves. I had a bigfoot shirt as well, but mine had daisies instead of the leaves. I was glad I hadn't picked that one.

"Great minds." I pointed.

"Can't go wrong with Neal Barney."

"I hope he is out there today."

"I think I saw he was supposed to be," Sawyer said.

We waited on Vee like always. She was high maintenance when it came to her appearance, but she was a laid-back person.

I was nearly out of patience when she finally came huffing down the stairs.

"Sorry, hair." She pointed. "It's a frizzy mess today."

"Ah, the joys of curly hair." I said. "Thank goodness mine is straight as a board."

"Me too." Sawyer flipped his hair.

His hair was black, straight like mine, and cut to about his jawline. Poor Vee had super curly red hair. She struggled with it and often just tried to secure it into some kind of ponytail or bun. Today, it was frizzy and not under control at all.

"Want me to help you?" I offered.

"Yes, can you?" She whined.

"Of course. I've been helping you for nearly thirty years."

We trekked back up to Vee's bathroom and grabbed her straightener, plugging it in, then grabbed some mousse and began working that into her hair. I used the straightener on her hair, pulling it through and curling each section for softer curls.

Over the years of friendship, I had learned how to do her hair for her. She never had the patience to learn for herself. I didn't mind.

When I was done, she smiled at me in the mirror.

"You're the best. What would I do without you?"

"Probably be on your way to a children's birthday party to make balloon animals and tell jokes." I laughed.

"Ha, ha. Still not funny. You need a new joke." She frowned, then winked. She loved me.

"Yeah, I guess that one is a little stale."

We headed downstairs. Sawyer whistled when he saw her.

"Better. Jess is awesome."

"Yeah, I can cook, do hair, and can clean. I'm the total package."

"Yes, you are. We just need to find you the right guy that sees it." Vee laughed.

"What? And leave the two of you? Never."

We laughed.

"Ready to go?"

"Yep."

We stepped out into the bright mid-morning. It was humid today, but there was not a cloud in the sky. From our house, it was three blocks south and four blocks east to the Albert Dashwood Memorial Park. We walked along the sunshine dabbled streets, passing others as they gathered and made the same trek to the park.

As we neared the park, we could hear the music and voices. Soon we were elbow to elbow moving through the crowd as we all made our way to one of the town's favorite annual events.

Here in Dashwood, if you weren't in some type of art, you knew someone in the arts, and culinary arts counted, too. We had a big foodie scene here, which is where I fit in. However, I also really loved visual arts.

We arrived at the edge of the park and this quarter's festival looked bigger than normal. Each year, it seemed to grow as more and more people heard about it and the marketing took off online.

People would come from the surrounding areas.

"Wow, it's crowded." Sawyer mumbled.

I looked down at tiny Vee. I hooked my arm with hers, so we didn't lose her. Sawyer and I were both six feet tall. Actually, he was taller by five inches, so between the two of us, we could see over most people. Vee was barely five feet tall, so we often lost her.

I chuckled to myself as I thought we must look like Papa Bear, Mama Bear, and Baby Bear as we made our way to the first booth. It held handmade butcher block cutting boards and knife blocks.

I wasn't familiar with this vendor, so I definitely wanted to check them out. These were neat, but I had plenty of kitchen items.

Still, I could admire the skill it took to make each of these items. I fingered the sharp edge of a cleaver.

"Nice." I said to the crafter.

"Thanks, Chef."

"How did you know?"

"You are all the same." He winked.

I didn't know how to take that, so I took it as flattery. I smiled and we walked to the next booth. After about an hour of going from booth to booth, we reached the culinary arts booth from our high school. I found the familiar face of my teacher, mentor, and now dear friend.

"Mr. Jones!" I shouted over the crowd.

He turned to look. A smile spread across his face as recognition took over.

"Little Jessie, how are you?"

"Ha, you have always called me little. There is nothing little about me." I joked.

"Ah, but I remember the scared, yet rebellious sixteen-year-old that first joined my class. That is how you will always look to me."

"And you will always be my favorite teacher."

"I was at The Crock Pot the other day."

"You've been back since opening day?"

"Yes, of course. It is wonderful. You should be quite proud of yourself."

"Thank you. I didn't know you had come in. Next time, ask for me and I'll come say hi."

"Nah, I know you are busy." He smiled, then nodded towards his students. "We have a good group this year."

Their booth was selling baked goods. Each time was a slightly different theme, but baked goods always did the best. I mean, who doesn't like a bag full of yummy cookies?

"Oh, these look good." I eyed the various baked goods until I spied my favorite. "How much for these snickerdoodles?"

"Five dollars." The student said.

"I'll give you ten." I said with a wink.

I knew they did this as a fundraiser for competitions and extra equipment that wasn't supplied by the state.

The confused student looked over at Mr. Jones. He nodded.

"Thank you."

I took one from the bag to taste it.

"Oh, wow. Which one of you made these?"

"I did, Chef." A lanky blond girl in the back said.

I was a little surprised that she knew who I was, but then I saw the smile on Duncan Jones's face and knew he had bragged.

"Well, when you graduate, hit me up. I might just need an extra pastry chef, especially someone who can make a snickerdoodle this good."

She blushed and giggled with pride. "Thanks, Chef."

Sawyer and Vee bought some items, and then we moved on. Jewelry was the next booth and while it was stunning, it wasn't my thing. Vee, on the other hand, was in heaven.

She showed me piece after piece. I feigned interest in the jewelry, but it just wasn't of interest. In the end, she bought three necklaces and two pairs of earrings.

As we started to walk to the next booth, a sarcastic voice came from behind me.

"Well, well, well. If it isn't my favorite chef."

"Hello, Flora. Good to see you."

"Is it?" She laughed.

"Of course. I have nothing against you. You're the one who has a problem with me."

She laughed a manic laugh. "You ready to give me a job, then?"

"As a busser, dishwasher, or maybe a server. Unless you have suddenly gotten kitchen experience."

"No." She folded her arms hard across her chest, glaring at me.

"So, do you have art here today? I'd love to see it." Maybe flattery would soften her attitude towards me.

"I do. It's at a booth over there." She gestured to the ones across from us. "You probably can't afford anything I have for sale though, seeing as you spent so much on that crappy business of yours."

My mouth nearly fell open. She had been begging to work at my *crappy* business, and now she was insulting it.

"Um, I'm sure you don't know what I spent on it."

"Well, I could guess."

"What is your problem?" Vee said at my side.

"Where is your mother, little girl?" Flora laughed.

Vee took a step forward, which Flora wasn't expecting. It caused her to take a step back.

"Ladies, that's enough." Sawyer said. "Look, we'll go our way, you go yours, and neither the two shall meet. Okay?"

"Whatever you say, grandpa." She laughed as she walked away.

As I watched her walk into the crowd, I saw her wave to a familiar face. That looked like one of my bussers.

"Hey, that's Eric. One of my employees." I pointed as I saw the two hug. As their hug ended, she said something to him, and he looked around. His face turned beet red when he saw me, and he suddenly ducked into the crowd.

"What was that about?" Vee asked.

"I think I might know who my mole is?" I grabbed my phone and shot a text message to Noah. He should still be at the restaurant.

As I waited for his reply, we moved to the next booth. It came roughly ten minutes later.

N: **What the heck?**

Me: **I know! I'm not sure what to think.**

N: **Have you seen him again?**

Me: **No, but I might walk over to her booth to see if he is there.**

N: **Let me know. We might have to let him go**

Me: **Sadly yes. I hate interviewing.**

N: **I'll handle it all. Less stress for you**

Me: **You're the best. I'll keep you posted**

Sawyer smiled at me. I think he could read my mind but didn't say anything. Vee seemed to skip along with us, happy as a clam to just be out and shopping.

We made our way around a few more booths before finding ourselves at Flora's booth. Her art was amazing. It was the eyes for me. They were so realistic it was almost like looking into the soul of the image.

I studied one of an elven child. The innocence, a hint of mischief with a side of playfulness she captured in his eyes was magical. I wanted to reach out and touch him.

"Ah, I thought we were going to stay out of each other's way. What happened?" She said to my right. I hadn't seen her walk up but wasn't surprised.

"I love your art. I just wanted to see more of it."

"Well, as I said, you couldn't possibly afford one of mine. They are far too expensive."

"Did Eric tell you that?"

"No, we don't talk about you. He's just a friend."

"Okay," I turned towards the elf child. "How much is this beauty?"

"Three-fifty." She scoffed.

The canvas was roughly 20 inches tall by 18 inches wide. I had just the place for it in my room. He could greet me each morning with his sweet, slightly mischievous smile.

"I'll take him."

Her mouth fell open. She looked over her shoulder at it and then back at me.

"Are you serious?"

"Yeah, I love him. Did you name him?"

"Um, no … I didn't."

"I think I'll call him Luca." I smiled at my friends. "Does that suit him?"

"He does look like a Luca." Vee chirped.

"Oh, well, okay." Flora stammered. "Do you want me to wrap him in brown paper? That's usually what I do."

I nodded as I fought a smirk.

I think I had put her off balance, and she didn't know how to react now. Good, I was glad to have a leg up this time.

She wrapped up the print and smiled at me.

"Wow, I've been so awful to you and here you'll have one of my paintings."

"Yeah, I have the perfect place for it in my room. Luca will greet me each morning."

She made a startled, happy sound, and then I scanned my card through her reader.

"Well, you're all set. Thank you so much for this. I haven't sold many." She confessed.

"Do you have a website or place I can put a review?"

"Oh, yes, um, of course." She grabbed a business card and handed it to me. "I really appreciate it."

"Let me know if you paint him a sister or a friend. I would be interested in a pair."

"I will. I actually have an idea for one but haven't gotten her painted yet."

"I look forward to it."

I walked away with my new painting, and my head held high. When we were a few booths away, I saw Eric. His eyes went wide as we made eye contact.

"Hi, Chef." He mumbled, looking past me. Probably looking for Flora.

"Hi, Eric. I just bought a painting from your friend Flora."

"Oh, yeah, she does good … um … art."

"Wanna tell me about how you know each other?"

"Um, no. I mean, we're just friends. I don't know her very well."

"Okay." I looked him up and down. We were nearly the same height. I didn't know if I believed his story about only being casual friends, but I was going to let it go for now. "See you at work."

I stormed off quickly, trying to outrun my anger, but in doing so I almost forgot about my friends. Reaching the edge of the park, I turned back to see poor Vee's legs just pumping. Thankfully, Sawyer had stayed with her, though he could have easily kept up with me.

"Sorry. I didn't know what to say to him." I said when they caught up to me. "I panicked and ran."

"I know." Vee said, slightly out of breath. "He looked guilty as heck."

"Do you think he has been helping her vandalize and torture you?" Sawyer asked.

"Yeah, I do think so. Maybe it isn't Jenn at all, but him. Though not sure how he would have all the passwords or know how to do that computer stuff? He had mentioned he didn't have much experience in anything."

"That could be a lie."

"Obviously … or probably. Ugh, I hate this." I fought the urge to punch something. I was not normally a violent person. "I just want to cook. Why did I want to be the boss again?"

Vee wrapped her arms around me, which was quite a feat considering we were both loaded down with our finds for the day.

"So, are y'all ready to go?" Sawyer asked.

"Yeah, what do y'all want for dinner? I'm cooking."

"Do you have time to make that rosemary chicken with the little potatoes?" Vee asked, biting her lip.

"Yeah, let's drop this stuff at home and then I can head over to the store."

"I'll go with you." Sawyer said. "I need to pick up a few things."

"Me too!" Vee smiled.

"Alrighty, it's a plan."

Chapter Nineteen

After dinner, I hung up my new painting. Luca would be the first and last thing I would see each day. His face calmed me.

However, I was a bit paranoid, so I checked it over to make sure that Flora hadn't placed some bug or camera on it when I wasn't paying attention. Can't be too careful with my safety after this person has been harassing me.

When I woke up the next morning, he was the first thing I saw. It made me smile.

"Good morning, Luca." I said.

His slightly wicked smile greeted me. I could just picture his bubbly sing-song voice telling me good morning in return.

As I was enjoying my morning coffee, my phone alerted. It was the alarm again at the restaurant. I pulled up the app so I could check the cameras. I scrolled through all of them but didn't see anything.

What the bleep?

The alarm company called, and it was the same story. It went off but reset on its own.

"What could be causing that?" I asked.

"Could be a spider on the sensor or could be a problem with the equipment." The representative said.

"Well, how do I know which one?"

"We just need to wait to see if it happens again."

"It has happened several times. It wakes me up at night. Isn't there a record or something on my account?"

"No, we don't keep that."

"Seriously? Then how do you track if there is a problem?"

That didn't seem like good business practice. Is that why Jenn picked this provider? I was going to have to research a new company. The thought of that gave me a headache.

"Do you think there is a problem?" The representative asked.

"Yes."

"We can send a rep out to look at the equipment."

"Thank you. Yes, please."

"Okay, we can get someone out ... Let's see ... umm ... On the 5th at noon."

"That's two weeks away and we are a restaurant. Noon is right in the middle of the lunch rush."

"I can do July eighteenth. At eight a.m."

"Wow, that's more than a month away. So, you are telling me those are the only available times?"

"Yes, at least until August, then we have a few times."

I counted to ten in Spanish to calm myself. It always worked, but this time I should have gone to twenty or maybe one hundred.

"I'll have to call you back."

"Okay, but our appointments fill up fast."

I'm not surprised given the poor quality, but I would keep that to myself. We hung up, and I laid my head on the kitchen island to ground myself.

Part of me was screaming about how Jenn bought this subpar security system because they were easy to hack. It was so obvious to me now.

But the other part wanted to give her the benefit of the doubt. Perhaps it wasn't an intentional thing. Maybe, just maybe, she didn't realize they had such bad service.

Frustration at the phone call had me wanting to scream into the silence, but my roommates were still asleep. That would be rude. Instead, I finished my coffee and breakfast, then went to get ready for work.

As I was getting ready, the alarm went off again and again; it reset per the following telephone call. This time, I simply thanked the representative and decided to go in early.

I was going to see if I could look at that camera myself. Not that I thought I could fix it, but if there was a spider or bug or maybe dust, I could fix that at least.

I sent a text to Noah. Hopefully, he could come in early so we could talk about the next steps with Eric and Jenn. Plus, this stupid security system. What was I going to do with it?

I headed out, arriving more than an hour early. Parking in the empty lot, I walked around the entire building, looking at all sides of the restaurant. There was no graffiti or damage that I could see.

We didn't have windows that opened, but we had three exit doors, so I checked each one. Plus, I looked at the areas around each external camera. Even though none of these were acting up, it was worth looking at them.

When I was satisfied with the outside inspection, I headed in. I turned off the alarm, then turned on the lights. My beautiful oasis calmed me.

As I walked through to the office, I started checking equipment and prep stations, just to see how the closing went last night. I had to do inspections from time to time to ensure that we were keeping things clean and maintained, anyway.

Plus, was something loose that was causing the sensor to go off. I didn't find anything and everything looked good.

Next, I entered the supply closet and took a two-step ladder and a microfiber towel to the malfunctioning camera. Since I was six-feet tall, the extra two and a half feet put the camera at nearly eye level with me. It gave me a good look at the camera.

First, I did a visual inspection of the camera and then wiped the towel around it. I studied the towel a bit more to see if there was a spider or something. A bit of dust, but nothing else and not a lot of dust at that. Arlo kept the restaurant's non-cooking equipment clean and tidy.

"So, weird." I mumbled.

The back door opened.

"Morning, Jess." Noah called out as he came in. He was followed closely by Arlo.

"Oh, good morning. Hi, Arlo."

"Chef." He nodded. "Anything specific you need done?"

"I haven't checked the closing log yet, but did you get that one sink fixed in the restroom?" I climbed down the two steps. Arlo stepped over to take the ladder from me.

"I had to pick up a part." He held up a bag. "It's on my list for the day."

"Great. Did you give the receipt to Noah?" I gestured.

"Yep, I already got it from him." Noah patted his pocket.

"Perfect. Are you ready to chat?"

He nodded and went into the office. I threw my purse in the usual place while he turned on the computer with only a slight thought about what could happen to it while I worked.

"So, how many times has this thing gone off on you?"

"I have lost count. About three times this morning though."

"And you said you called, but they couldn't come out until July?"

"Yes, well, they can come on the 5th at noon, but that is the same as not coming. Noon at a restaurant is not going to happen."

He pulled up the cameras so we could review the security footage together. We went to around the time we both left yesterday. It was mostly just Jenn doing a little paperwork, and then she left the office for a while. It was around dinner service, so I'm sure she was out assisting the servers and hosts.

The office was empty for a few hours, so I pulled up a side window with the dining room camera. We could see nearly every table was full. Nothing crazy happened and the office was empty the entire time she was out front.

Once things started to slow, she returned to the office. We could see her run the evening reports, making a few notes on them, filing them away. Then she checked her phone.

Tyler came to the door, said something to her, then they both left. We saw them come out into the dining room; she spoke to a customer. My mind went to a dark place until I realized they were all smiling.

"Oh, good. I was worried something was wrong for a minute." Noah said.

"Yeah, I was concerned for a second, too."

"I know not everyone will like the food, but overall, we haven't had many bad comments or reviews."

"I know. It is shocking." I chuckled.

"Not really, you have done a good thing here, Chef." He smiled.

"*We* did a good thing."

He chuckled. "We have."

Nothing really exciting happened at all. We watched long after the time she shut off the lights. Around one a.m., there was a flicker, but nothing showed on the camera.

"What was that?" I asked.

"I didn't see anything."

"Back it up about a minute."

He tapped a few buttons with the mouse.

"Okay, watch closely. It flickers a bit … Now."

"Oh, wow. I did see that. I might need to have Colt check this part out."

"Has he looked at the rest of what you sent him yet?"

"Yes, he did confirm it was edited, and he is trying to see if he can hack into the security company to see if they have the unedited files."

My mouth fell open at his words. He said it as casually as if he had commented on the weather.

"He is hacking into the company." I choked out.

"Yeah. You wanted answers. Colt can get them."

"That's unethical."

"What? You want to wait on Mr. Detective who can't seem to find any clues for a murder that seems so straightforward! Earl was shot right out there." Noah's nostrils flared. "Why haven't they checked the surrounding business's cameras? They looked at ours, but I have heard nothing about the others."

"We don't know that he hasn't checked those cameras."

"True, but wouldn't they have seen something, found something. I mean they said they caught the car on the edge of our camera. So wouldn't the eye doctor across from us or the barber next to them have something."

I had no answers for that, and I knew he was frustrated and upset about this situation. I was too, but I didn't know what to do. It wasn't like I had experience in how to navigate all of this.

We didn't learn about what-to-do-when-your-sous-chef-is-killed-by-your-dumpster classes in culinary school. We had food safety or learned about knife skills, but police work, not so much.

I was doing this on the fly and not doing it well. I had my business to run, food to cook, and employees to keep track of. Investigating murder was not top of my list of to-dos. I had a naïve faith in the police, despite my history with them.

However, I also knew that hacking into a company was unethical and not something I could knowingly sign off on.

"Well, the suspects keep coming up with credible alibis. And I am just as upset as you are, but I'm not sure hacking is the right move." I paused. "However, just don't tell me how you find answers. Just do it."

A slow smile spread across his face. "Alright. I'll check with him. Now, we need to discuss Jenn and Eric."

"I just don't see anything but poor judgment on Jenn's part in this. She hasn't given me any reason to think she is involved."

He frowned. "Yeah, maybe not, especially after what you said about Eric. I mean, any of the employees can get in after hours."

"And she explained the strange vendor. Our regular one wasn't available, so she had to use that one a few times."

"Yeah, she did."

All the employees had an individual number that turned off the alarm. We didn't do one main number so that when we let people go, we could just deactivate that one and not have to change it each time.

Now that we were looking at letting go of one of the employees, it was going to be put to the test. If nothing else happened inside the restaurant, then we would know for sure it was Eric and that Jenn wasn't involved.

"But I do have concerns that he isn't smart enough to know how to do this." Noah said.

"Yes, but he could easily let someone in that could."

"That's true."

I just couldn't go there thinking that one of my most trusted employees was doing this to me. She had direct access to our bank accounts, the safe, and all the employees' personal information. It was unfathomable to me that she could be involved.

Eric, on the other hand, had been acting strange the last couple of weeks. He often would stand watching me while I worked or would show up in weird places, like behind me. It was almost like he was stalking me, though it could just be an odd coincidence.

"Since Eric has been acting off and the servers are starting to complain, plus he was with Flora yesterday, I think we should let him go," Noah said.

I groaned. "I know we need to."

"I know that's the part of the job you hate, so I will handle all of it. Also, I think you and I need to shop around for a new security company."

"Yes, I think so too. Does your friend have any recommendations?"

"I'll ask him about which ones have the toughest systems to hack, and he would know." Noah added a wink to the end.

"That doesn't make it sound creepy at all."

He chuckled.

"Alright, so we have a plan?" I asked.

"What about Jenn?"

"Let's just keep an eye on her and once we switch systems, it won't matter. At least that part of it."

"Okay, you're the boss."

"You don't agree?"

He sighed. "I do, but I think I am just paranoid. Let's get rid of Eric and the security system, then see how things go. In the meantime, let's hope the detective can come up with something."

I nodded and went to prep for the day. Noah was going to handle everything else. I stopped in my tracks.

Wait? Should I put all this trust in Noah? That nagging thought crept back into my mind. He had a friend who could hack into companies. What did that say about him?

I looked over my shoulder at the office door. He couldn't see me from here. Well, unless he was still looking at the cameras. I smiled and continued to my station, but if he wanted us to keep an eye on Jenn, I was going to watch him.

Chapter Twenty

At the end of day shift, Noah called Eric to the back office and fired him. I didn't get to hear what was said, but I saw the aftermath of him storming out of the office, cursing his head off.

I was so thankful to have Marco around as he was not only one of my bussers, but in a pinch, he could be a security guard. This was the second time we'd needed him.

He came into the kitchen when he heard the ruckus and then escorted Eric to the door. All eyes watched Marco throw the back door open and shove Eric out.

"You'll be sorry for this! All of you!" Eric spat out. "You don't know who I am or who you are messing with!"

Marco let the door slam in his face.

I exhaled and looked around. Everyone was looking at me.

"Sorry, y'all. It was time."

"No worries, Chef."

"He has been slacking recently."

"Scary stuff, but we got your back."

"We love you, Chef."

I smiled, then nodded for Noah to join me in the office. Jenn hadn't yet arrived, but would soon, so before she did, I just wanted to touch base with him once more.

"Wow, that was explosive." I said as we sat.

"You should have been in here with him." Noah coughed. "I'm glad he is gone."

"Did you already disable his security code?"

"I did before I called him back. I have also made it so only you and I are the only ones that can make changes to employee codes going forward."

"Okay." I didn't know how Jenn would take that, but it didn't matter, I had to protect my business.

"I also talked to the bank and increased our security, moving most of our assets to another account."

"Oh, thanks. I hadn't thought of that."

"Yeah, I just left enough to pay bills."

"I have to think of how I'm going to frame these changes to Jenn."

"What changes?" a voice at the door said. It was Jenn.

"Oh, hey." Ready or not, I had to have one of those difficult conversations I hated. "Yeah, we have had to make some changes but get settled and I'll explain."

Hopefully that will buy me some time to think of what I should say.

"I'm ready." She dropped her purse on the desk and plopped hard into the third chair. "What's up?"

Well, darn, I had hoped for more than two seconds to prepare my thoughts.

"We had to let Eric go." I started.

"Yeah, we have started to get complaints about him. It was time."

She didn't even bat an eye, which further confirmed my thoughts that she didn't have anything to do with this.

"Yes, and because of letting him go, plus everything else going on, we have added some security measures to our banking and security system."

"Oh." She looked at each of us. "Meaning?"

"Meaning Noah and I are the only ones who can access the employee codes, edit or add those, and we have limited some of your banking access." I said, wincing when I saw her face fall.

"You think I have something to do with this?" Tears formed in her eyes, and I instantly felt guilty.

"No, not at all. We just want to keep things a little tighter until some of this stuff passes. Then we are hoping to return things to normal."

She grabbed a tissue, wiping her eyes. "Okay. I wouldn't do that to you. Just so you know."

"I know."

At least I wanted to believe it, but I looked at Noah. His body language screamed that he didn't seem to believe it, but he simply smiled at her.

"Is there anything else?" she asked, sniffling.

"No, just that. Nothing major and you should still be able to do your job."

"Okay." She looked at Noah. "So, I guess business as usual. We can do our touch base before you leave?"

"Absolutely." He nodded.

"Well, I'm going to check in with June and Parker before I leave and then head out." I grabbed my purse so that I wouldn't have to come back to say goodbye to them.

"Have Marco walk you out?" Noah suggested.

"Oh, thanks. I will."

An hour later, I was at home prepping dinner for my friends. I thought I would surprise them with baked chicken, garlic smashed potatoes and roasted brussels sprouts.

Cooking was my love language, and it brought me such joy. Though there were times, it was nice to go out and not have to cook after doing it all day.

I had the chicken seasoned and in the oven, when Sawyer and Vee came in. The positive energy they brought to the house warmed my heart. It was one of the million reasons why we were friends. They always made me so extremely happy even when I have had a miserable day.

"Hi, honey, I'm home." Sawyer burst into the kitchen. He wrapped me in a huge hug.

"Aw, hi, babe." I laughed.

"Something smells good in here." Vee chirped at his side.

"Roast chicken, potatoes, and brussels sprouts."

"Oh, are you doing those crispy, garlicky potatoes?" Sawyer asked, looking around me at the stove.

They were boiled first to soften them, then I would lay them on a cookie sheet, smashing them slightly before slathering them in garlic, salt, black pepper, and melted butter. Then they were roasted to crispy perfection. I knew my roommates both loved them.

"Yep, those very ones."

"Those are the *beeest*!"

"What did we do to deserve such an amazing cook as our friend?" Vee giggled.

"You're just lucky." We laughed. "Now, go change and wash up for dinner, children." I teased and shooed them out of the kitchen so I could finish up.

Once dinner was ready, I plated for each of them and set it on the table.

"Bon Appetit." We said together.

We all dug in. It was heavenly. After all this time, I was still surprised by my skills in the kitchen. It was so fun to take various ingredients and make something warm and wonderful.

They chatted about a day in the life of a postal worker, comparing notes.

Sawyer was enjoying his move from the customer service desk to loading trucks and sorting in the back. Vee still worked at the desk, and her job was mostly taking packages and selling the odd postage stamp.

She said fewer and fewer people bought them. I believed her because I can't even remember the last time I needed a stamp.

"Jess, you're so quiet. You okay?" Vee asked.

She was intuitive and always seemed to sense my negative mood. She was into yoga, Zen, and meditating. Her energy and vibe were always calming and peaceful in nature.

"We let Eric go today, and it did *not* go well."

"Oh, wow. You said you thought it might go that way."

"Yeah, Marco had to almost throw him out. Not gonna lie, I fully expect something to happen tonight."

"Really?" Sawyer said around a mouth full of potato.

"With the security system acting up though, it will be difficult to know what is real and what isn't."

"What are y'all doing about that?" Vee asked.

"Noah is researching new ones."

"Do you think you can trust him?"

I fought the urge to shout out in his defense but also scream in my paranoia. I didn't know anymore who I could trust, but I really did feel like he was being sincere.

"I want to, and I feel like I can, but honestly, I am feeling super paranoid about everyone and everything. I almost want to give up the restaurant and go back to just being a chef for someone else."

"No! You've worked too hard for this."

"You can't do that!"

"But ... *but* I don't want to. You're right, I have worked extremely hard to get here, so I have to trust some people along the way. I *think* I can trust Noah and, more than anything, I want to."

Nobody said anything as we all began eating again. The only sound was the clink of the forks against the plates, the hum of the fridge, or soft chewing sound. There wasn't much else to say.

Sawyer, of course, finished his meal first and got a second plate full. Vee got a few more potatoes. I knew they were her favorite, so I made them at least once a month for her, sometimes more. I'd also added them to The Crock Pot's menu in honor of her.

"Jessie, this was amazing, as always." Sawyer said as he finished his second plate. "I've got cleanup."

He started grabbing our plates and heading into the kitchen. We could hear him moving around.

Vee and I moved into the living room. She curled up almost like a cat in one corner of the couch, her feet tucked under her. I sat stretched out in the other corner.

I flipped through the channels until we found a crime drama. It was a rerun, but it was the perfect comfort show to watch tonight. Sawyer joined us, sitting in his favorite spot on the oversized chair.

We sat in comfortable silence, watching television until my phone rang. It was my Granny Ines. She rarely called on Mondays.

"Hi, Granny Ines."

"Jessie, mija, I have sad news. Your father was in a fight or attacked. I didn't understand who they said started things. He's in the infirmary." Her voice cracked.

"What? Are you serious?" My heart sank as I remembered him mentioning he had received threats. He had seemed unconcerned about it.

"Yes, he is okay, I think. Broken nose and stabbed in the shoulder and stomach. They said no visitors for a few days, so I want to go on Thursday. Can you go with me?"

Stabbed? She said it so casually; I wasn't sure if I heard her correctly.

"He was stabbed? How is that possible? I thought they couldn't have anything sharp."

I saw my roommates sit forward at my words.

"Contraband knife or something. I didn't understand how they said that it happened exactly, I was too shocked, but I do know they said he would be okay. He just needed to stay in the infirmary for a few days."

"Okay." I mumbled.

My mind was spinning. I didn't have the best relationship with him, but he was still my father, and I had five wonderful years of memories together. Though I couldn't remember the first few, I know I was loved.

"You didn't answer about going with me."

"I will see if someone can cover my shift, but yes, if I can get that covered."

"Jessie, aren't you the boss? Can't you just *take off*?"

"No, unfortunately, that's not how it works. People depend on me to be there."

"If you say so. Just let me know if you will go with me."

"I will Granny Ines, and please let me know if you hear anything else about him."

"Love you, Mija."

"I love you, too."

With that, we hung up. I stared at the phone for a second, then looked over at my friends. They were staring at me.

"What happened?" Vee asked.

"Dad was stabbed and has a broken nose."

"Oh my gosh, is he okay?"

"She said he would be."

"Are you going to see him?" Sawyer asked.

"She wants us to go on Thursday."

"Do you need us to go with you?"

While that would be a comfort to me, I would be with my grandmother and probably my aunt would go to. Despite my grandmother being a touch gruff, she loved me and cared for me all my life.

"No, I mean, this isn't the first time he has gotten into a scrap. It probably won't be the last."

Though this was the first time I felt responsible for his situation. I'd need to go to clear my conscience.

Chapter Twenty-One

I stared at the text message. Vivian, Earl's mother, wanted to come see me. After all this time, I hadn't heard from her. Why now? I just had a sick feeling in the pit of my stomach about facing her, and I couldn't explain why.

I replied I would be at the restaurant until three. She could come then, or we could meet somewhere else. She replied she would be here at quarter to three.

That was just before opening today, and it had been a cloud over my head all day. I had three separate orders sent back because of my inattention to details today. I could scream with frustration and worry about what Vivian was coming to say to me.

I felt responsible for his death and my inability to find the killer which wasn't even my job to do, but I still felt it deep in my soul. How could I look at her and not give her answers?

Jordan came back at exactly 2:45 to let me know Vivian had arrived.

"Thank you. Ask her if she would like anything, on the house, of course, and I will be with her shortly."

"Yes, Chef." Jordan returned to the dining room while I washed up. I smiled at my kitchen staff as I took a deep breath, then went to greet her.

"Hi, Vivian. Nice to see you," I said as cheerfully as possible. I took a seat across from her at the booth.

"Hi, Jess. It has been a minute." She smiled but quickly frowned again. "I wish I were here on pleasant business."

Jordan brought over an iced tea for Vivian and a lemonade for me.

"I'm sorry to hear it isn't a friendly visit. I have missed seeing you." That was true.

I saw her often when Earl and I worked together, especially when he was still in culinary arts school. She would drop him off and pick him up each day.

"Well, I received this." She passed her phone to me. The display showed her text messaging. The text read.

Chef Jessica got your son killed. She is evil and selfish. Together, we can destroy her. Will you help us?

My eye bugged out of my head.

"Vivian, I didn't … I loved … you don't believe….?" I couldn't seem to form full sentences. It was frustrating.

She took my hand.

"No, Jess, I don't believe this, and I have no idea who would say such things. I know you and Earl had a special friendship. He looked up to you." She whipped out a tissue from her purse, delicately dabbing her eyes.

"Then why bring this to me?"

"I thought I should warn you about this person. I mean, I have no idea who it is, but clearly whoever it is, they aren't finished."

"We should show the police, especially Detective Upton."

"Ha, that's rich. Those buffoons can't even figure out who killed my son nearly three months ago. They don't even have any leads. Just keep telling me they are working on it. The only thing they are getting close to is another dead body, because between the person who killed Earl, then shot at us, and now this, these people will not stop." She had kept her voice even, but it was clear she was discouraged and scared.

I was too, and I knew she was right, but I still didn't know what to do. I had little spare time to investigate and all my asking around, looking, and trying to figure this out had gotten me nowhere fast.

Each time I talked to the Detective, he would give me half stories and just tell me the suspects had alibis. Nothing solid enough to stick. But had they checked cameras on neighboring businesses, like Noah had said? I didn't know. Had they even followed up on the alibis? I didn't know, even though he had said they did. Did they really?

I am down an employee now because of this and hurting another with our paranoia. I had no real reason to suspect Jenn.

"Do you have any ideas at all who could be doing this?" I asked her.

"I have long suspected his old roommate. There was something shady about him."

"Silas?"

"No, the one before that. Silas might know him. They used to all be friends. Used to hang out before I pulled Earl out of that school and put him in Duncan Jones's culinary school. That straightened Earl out. No more burglary for him."

That was the first time I had heard he was a burglar. It made sense though, because a lot of us ended up in Mr. Jones's class for that reason. I mean I'd stolen a car, but just my stepfather's car. That shouldn't count.

"Okay, I'll go talk to Silas again. See if he knows anything about the old roommate. What's his name?"

"Reggie something or other. I can't remember, but Silas will know him."

I nodded. I hesitated to ask her the next question because it would be admitting that I snooped in his room, but I needed answers.

"I'm sorry to ask this, because honestly it is none of my business and I have no right to know about it." I took a deep breath. "I found a bank statement in his room when I went there a few weeks ago, he had a lot of money. Was he doing something ... um, illegal or something?"

"Oh, gosh, no. He had been saving to buy a food truck. That was until he got the job working for you. Then he put that on hold. He figured he could always do it in the future if he wanted."

"Oh, wow. I had no idea." That explained the large sum in his account. "I didn't mean to snoop, but I was just worried about what could have happened."

"I understand." She smiled.

"He would have been a great food truck owner. I'm sorry he never had the chance." My voice cracked.

We hugged, then she took a long sip of her iced tea before saying goodbye. I promised to keep in touch.

"I'll let you know if I find out anything."

"Be safe, Jess. Earl wouldn't want you hurt for him."

"Yeah, well, I would have taken a bullet for him." I tried to smile, but a lump had formed in my throat.

She hugged me again, then walked out. I stared at the door for a moment, letting the conversation sink in.

Damn, someone was threatening me through her. It was creepy and not at all flattering.

I went back to the kitchen to finish my shift and turn over the place to June for the night. I drove home with a heavy sense of dread.

The radio was an okay distraction, so I cranked it loud, trying to sing along, but my mind wouldn't stay in the song.

My mind kept asking questions that again, I had no answers to. Unless I figured out who was behind all of this, I would never know and would always be looking over my shoulder.

The urgency to figure this out was getting overwhelming.

The first thing I did when I got home was send a text message to Silas.

Me: **You working?**

S: **Nah. What's up?**

Me: **Can you meet me for a beer at Dragon's Alley? On me.**

S: **Yep, time?**

Me: **6**

S: **See ya then**

Okay, now to talk Sawyer and Vee into going with me. They loved Dragon's Alley, so it wouldn't be hard. It would give me a couple of hours to decide what to ask and how to ask so not to give too much away. I didn't know if this Reggie person was still friends with Silas or if he was involved. Would Silas be loyal to Earl or Reggie? I had no idea. Either way, I had to protect myself.

A few hours later, Sawyer, Vee, and I were sitting in Dragon's Alley waiting on Silas. They had been easy to talk into coming. We all ordered a beer.

Our waiter brought them over just as Silas arrived.

He did the head nod thing when he spotted me, then made his way to our table.

"Hey, y'all." He said. Since the waiter was still at the table, he ordered a beer. "Glad you messaged, Jess. It's been a while. How are you?"

"I'm good. How are you?"

"Oh, you know, busy most of the time. Can't seem to find another roommate worth a damn since Earl. That guy was solid."

"Yeah, he has been difficult to replace."

"I did hear you got a new sous chef that has been working out well over there."

"Oh, yeah, who did you hear that from?"

"Word gets around Dashwood." He laughed. I frowned, so he added. "Nobody really, just word on the street."

"Yeah, I always forget at times how fast news travels." I twirled the straw in my drink.

The waiter brought his beer. "Y'all ready to order?"

"Um, give us another minute or two."

"Take your time. I'm here all night." He chuckled and then left us.

We quietly looked over the menus. I didn't know how to start this conversation yet, so I didn't mind the slight distraction. A few moments later, the waiter came to take our order, then once he was gone, I couldn't stall any longer and got to the business of this meeting.

"So, you mentioned roommates before. Do you know Earl's former roommate?"

"Oh, sure, Reggie. You know him too."

"I do?"

"Yeah, he said he interviewed to be a chef for you."

"Reggie?" I thought, then the lightbulb went off. "Oh, I remember him."

"He's a bit of a hothead and thinks he is better at things than he is."

I chuckled, "That was my impression of him."

"Yeah, I was friends with him, but after one too many fights and drama, I haven't spoken to him in years."

"How do you know he interviewed with me?"

"I ran into him recently. We were talking about Earl's death, and he mentioned he interviewed for you."

I nodded.

"Oh, he might have been the one who told me you hired someone. Anyway, is that why you wanted to talk to me, about him?"

"Yeah, a little. Someone had mentioned his former roommate might know something about who killed him, and I wasn't sure who that was."

"Ah, well, there you go. Answer is Reggie Reardon." He smiled. "If it helps find out who killed my bud, I will help in any way."

"That's how I feel too."

Our food arrived, so our focus turned to eating and conversation changed to video games, art, and movies. Sawyer and

Silas had a lot of the same interests, so they bonded while Vee and I mostly listened.

It was a nice evening with friends.

As we were leaving, Silas turned to me.

"Did you have any other questions?"

"Um, do you know who Reggie hangs out with?"

"Not really. We haven't been friends in so long, and we don't run in the same circles any longer. Like I said, I just ran into him randomly. I doubt I'll see him again, unless it is a random bump in again."

"Thanks. Well, if you think of anything, please let me know."

"I will." He turned to leave. "Oh, and hey, don't be a stranger. I like y'all. We should hang out more."

"Definitely."

"You got it, man. We need to hop online to play together." Sawyer said. They did a bro hug. Vee and I roll our eyes at each other with a laugh.

With that, we parted ways.

"Do you feel like you got your answers?" Vee asked once we were on the road.

"I guess. I mean, I needed to know who his former roommate was, and I found that out. He was the hothead I told you we had to throw out before we hired June."

"Oh, that was the roommate?" Vee gasped. "Yikes. So maybe Vivian is on to something with being suspicion of him."

"Yeah, maybe. He definitely seemed to have a reason to hate me, but he wasn't even on my radar of suspects. I have been so focused on Flora, but mostly because she has been so open in her hate and had accepted the blame for spraying my restaurant."

"Yes, she seems like the easiest one to blame, but the easiest doesn't always mean that's the one." Sawyer said.

He was always logical. It was something I had to think about.

Chapter Twenty-Two

Between the news of my father and the alarm going off randomly, I had another restless night. I decided to give up on getting any sleep.

I hadn't lost this much sleep over my father in a long time. I didn't like it. Could my life get back to normal, please?

I did my usual morning routine, but with a second cup of coffee, and I made a huge breakfast for my friends. I left it with a note from me, then headed to the restaurant early. Maybe I could work on the new soup recipe that's been on my mind. If it turned out, maybe it would be the special for the day.

Parking, I did a quick visual inspection on the exterior. Nothing out of the ordinary.

I sighed as I made my way to the back door, unlocking it, then typing in the alarm code. I flipped on the kitchen light. As my eyes adjusted to the change in light, I gasped at the horror in front of me.

"What in the freaking hell?"

Someone had trashed the kitchen. Equipment was thrown everywhere. Food had been pulled out of the fridge and freezer and was strewn from one end to the other.

I slowly walked through the nightmare before me. My heart sank with each step. It was a huge gut punch.

"What in the world happened?" I heard someone say behind me.

I turned to see Noah and Arlo standing in the doorway. It was actually a relief that they had both come in early today, too. Arlo was often here early to ensure everything was in working order and clean before we opened.

"I … don't even know, but I have a few guesses."

"Did you call the police?"

"Not yet. I only just got here myself, so I haven't even processed what this is." I gestured all around at the mess. My beautiful kitchen, my dream, had been destroyed.

"Chef, should I start to cleaning?" Arlo asked.

I studied the mess. We needed to be prepping for the day, but I knew we couldn't actually start cleaning this until after the police came.

"No, unfortunately, we must wait until the police come and investigate. I'll call them now."

I dialed 9-1-1 and relayed the information to the operator.

"I will dispatch officers to your location. Would you like me to stay on the line with you until they arrive?"

"Um, no, thanks."

We hung up and then I thought perhaps I should call Detective Upton directly to let him know. Not sure why, but I hesitated.

"What's wrong, Jess?" Noah asked. I guess my face gave me away.

"I want to call the detective, but he hasn't exactly been good at this or sharing information if he does have it. I don't know."

"Yeah, it feels like they are dragging this on."

I thought about Chief Stone's attitude towards me and perhaps it was seeping into the rest of the police department. I exhaled heavily.

"Ugh, I'll call him."

Dialing his number, my heartbeat faster. I hate all of this.

"Hello?"

"Detective Upton?"

"Yes. Oh, Chef Jessica. Hello."

"There is an issue at the restaurant. I already called in to 9-1-1 but thought I should let you know."

"What's going on?"

"Someone came in and trashed the place. Like everything is thrown around. Equipment. Food. Everything."

"Okay, I'll check in with the station and then head over."

We hung up.

Noah had gone into the office. I sent Arlo home.

"I'll call you when we can begin cleaning up. I will need everyone's help."

He nodded and left.

Next, I sent a group text message to my day shift to let them know we would have a delayed start, then deleted that message without sending it. Added my entire staff to the to field then typed that we would be closed until further notice. Tears stung my eyes as I hit send on that one.

Replies came in almost instantly. They were concerned, of course, but were asking a lot of questions. I decided I needed to give a bit more information.

Me: The restaurant has been vandalized, and the police are on their way. I will keep you all updated. We will need everyone's help in cleaning it once they clear us to do so. I will be in touch.

I heard the police sirens. Not sure that was necessary. Noah came out of the office with a sign he had printed out.

"The office is a mess, but I managed to get this made and printed. I'll post this on the doors. I have already put something on both our website and various social media sites."

"No details?"

"No, just like this." He flashed me the sign that simply said closed until further notice.

"We will get questions."

"Well, I think the police arriving will tip them all off that something big happened. Plus, it's a small town. Word will get out." He turned to head to the front door.

I went out the back door to meet the police officers. They were just getting out of their cars when I stepped out.

"Chef." Officer Rafferty greeted me with a nod.

"Raff. Thanks for coming."

"So, what do we have?" He asked, taking out a small notepad.

"It would be easier to just show you." I sighed, then led the way in.

Rafferty whistled as he took in the scene. "Wow, Jess. I am so sorry. Knowing you since middle school, you don't deserve this. Nobody deserves this."

"Thanks." I know it was meant to make me feel better, but it didn't.

Officer Tommy Roberts pulled out a camera and began taking pictures, while Officer Perez made a call to the forensic team.

I stood by helplessly as the officers got to work. Noah showed them the security cameras, but honestly, I knew they wouldn't find anything. I wanted to cry.

Sawyer sent me a text message asking how I was.

I guess word had got out, I thought.

Me: Not gonna lie, this sucks.

S: Sorry, girl. Extra big hugs from me and Vee.
Me: Thanks

There wasn't much else I could say. My phone continued going off as employees reacted to the news. It hadn't stopped since I sent the initial message informing them about the closure. I haven't sent another response yet, but what could I say? I had no words or news to share, so what was the point?

The back door opened and in strode Detective Upton. His stern look melted into shock when he saw the mess.

"Chef, I am sorry. This is not at all what I pictured. Are you okay?"

"I am … I don't know." I choked out.

Words wouldn't form as tears threatened to fall. I was not normally the crying type, but this was beyond me.

He put a firm hand on my shoulder. It wasn't overly personal, but it was oddly comforting.

"We will figure this out. I'm going to touch base with the officers. Why don't you have a seat in the office, and I'll come talk to you once I'm done out here?"

I nodded.

"Here. Have a seat, Jess." Noah said when I came in. He turned a chair over for me, wiping it with a towel.

I think I muttered thank you, but the words may not have formed. We sat in silence, waiting for word from the officers.

I saw that most of the mess in here was just papers thrown around. The computer and printer were really the only things not damaged in some way. It was so random.

My heart was heavy after hearing the news about my dad being stabbed. Now this. My body ached from the stress. The lump in my throat grew and my eyes were barely holding the tears back.

When was this nightmare going to be over? First, poor Earl, then Vivian and I were shot at. Next there was the graffiti. My dad gets stabbed, which may or may not be related. Then this.

My dream was slowly turning into a nightmare.

Tears slowly fell as I thought of each event and each piece of the puzzle that I was missing. I wanted to figure this out, but time was not my friend here. Plus, wasn't that the police department's job?

I thought of the possible suspects, Eric, Reggie, and Flora.

Flora had taken credit for harassing me and spray painting the building, but she didn't seem like she would kill Earl or shoot at someone. Of course, I didn't know her well enough to say that.

Then there was Reggie. I couldn't figure out how he could have gotten inside without help from someone. However, I guess if he broke into places back in high school, he could have figured out how to get in here.

Plus, my run in with him was after Earl was killed. His anger at me came when we ended his interview because he wasn't prepared. I had vowed not to waste any more time on interviews when it was clearly not a fit.

Still, my hunch on this one was Eric, but how had he gotten in? Maybe his code still worked. With the subpar security system we still had, it wouldn't surprise me.

"Are you thinking Eric did it, too?" Noah asked, breaking the silence.

"Yeah. Who else could it be?"

"I have the footage from yesterday pulled up and paused, in case they want to see it." He gestured towards the kitchen. "Of course there isn't any of all that."

I nodded as we continued waiting. My tears had stopped. Crying more would have to wait until I was alone. I couldn't show weakness. It wasn't becoming of the boss to break down like that.

Hours later, Detective Upton came to speak to us in the office.

"We are done."

"Okay."

"You can go ahead and straighten up, try to get back to normal."

I nodded, still not trusting myself to speak.

"Please know we are doing all we can to find out who is behind all of this."

"It was probably Eric Henley. I am almost positive." Noah said.

"Why would you say that?" Detective Upton asked.

"We fired him yesterday, and we escorted him out. I can show you the footage, but there isn't sound." Noah offered.

"Um, yeah, can I see it?"

Noah pulled up the security cameras.

"Okay, here goes." He hit play.

Detective Upton's face was unreadable as he watched. He had his notepad out, making notes, but that was the only sign he was into the video.

"Can we get a copy of this?" He asked when it was finished.

"Yes, of course."

Upton stepped into the hallway, signaling to one of the officers who came forward with a USB drive. I guess the detective wasn't as prepared today.

Noah took it, plugged it in, and then tapped and clicked.

"Alrighty, here you go." He handed them the drive. "I'll walk y'all out."

Sitting alone now, I stared for a few moments, trying to decide what to do. Finally, I sent a text to select employees to come in so we could begin cleanup. I didn't need everyone. Too many bodies would just get in the way, and I really didn't want all of them to see this.

It was bad enough that I saw it.

As the replies came in, I decided to get started.

Walking back into the kitchen, my stomach churned as the horrible sight hit me anew. I took several deep breaths as I dawned some gloves and began grabbing food, throwing it straight into the trash.

Noah came in and began doing the same. By the time Arlo had returned, we had put a solid dent in at least picking up most of the food and had filled three full bags.

Arlo started righting the equipment and wiping it all down, checking to ensure it all still worked.

Next to arrive were Parker and Marco.

"Holy moly, Chef! I'm… I'm speechless." Parker said.

They both jumped in.

The rumor about Parker was still on my mind, but he was a good worker, so I asked him in today. If I got a chance, I would pull him aside to discuss the gossip. I didn't believe it.

Within an hour, we had all eight employees here and made quick work of the cleanup. Nobody really talked except what was necessary to coordinate cleanup efforts. I knew I'd called in the right employees.

It was hours before we finally looked around, satisfied that we had gotten us back to square one. Noah put in a desperate call to the food vendor to see if we could get a rushed order and then another call to the kitchen supply company to see how quickly they could get glassware, plates, and glass measure cups.

Thankfully, there was enough to keep us going, but it would mean the dishwasher had to be on their game, quickly getting things washed and then back on the line.

Since it was after dinner time, I ordered everyone pizza. We settled into the bar area to decompress from the day.

"Sorry, Chef. This had to have been a shock this morning." Ripley said.

"Yeah, it was a sickening feeling."

"Any ideas?" Parker asked.

"Not yet. The police have all the information, so we will just have to wait."

"I bet it was Eric." Marco grumbled.

"Well, like I said, the police took the information, so we'll have to wait and see."

"They haven't done a good job of finding Earl's killer."

"Or whoever shot at you and Earl's mom."

"I know. I know, but we have to be patient. Detective Upton has assured me they are working on it."

Nobody argued, but I could tell by their tense posture and frowns, they didn't believe it any more than I did. I really needed to look at this case closer myself.

It took so much time to run the business and with the stupid alarm issues, it had taken more of my focus. But I was determined to figure out who was out to sabotage my business.

As everyone started to head out, I asked Parker to stay behind.

"Hey, so thanks for helping out today." I started.

"Of course, Chef. You have done so much for me."

"Which makes this hard for me to ask."

"Ohmygosh, are you firing me?"

"No, no. I just heard a rumor, and I wanted to find out if it was true."

"Oh, thank goodness. I love working here and have no plans to leave. You're amazing to work for and learn from. I am so thankful for this job."

"Really? So, you aren't looking for a new job?"

"No way. Is that the rumor?"

"Yeah. When you took off last week, people were saying that you were interviewing for other positions."

"No, never, Chef. Where else would I get the opportunities you have given me? I'm here for the long haul."

"Well, that's good to hear. I appreciate your hard work and positive attitude."

We parted ways then. I watched him leave. Glad that was handled. I hate to think, I almost added him to the suspect list. He was a huge asset here. Selfishly, I didn't want to waste my time training him for him to leave.

Chapter Twenty-Three

I slid my car to a stop in front of Granny Ines's house. I took a deep breath to steady my nerves. I wasn't ready for this visit or the guilt trip that Granny would put on me for not going to see my father more.

As it was, I didn't feel comfortable being away from the restaurant after what happened on Tuesday. We got things cleaned up and had to reorder most of our food.

I was so grateful to the vendor that they replaced all our food quickly, so we were able reopen the next day. I had to ask a number of my employees to come in early so we could get the food checked in and put away quickly, then prep for the day.

It came at a cost, but it was a small price to pay to get back to normal, but staying closed any longer than a day was not an option. Actually, it was a big price, but worth it.

When I was planning, I had worked everything to the penny for the first two years. I had a sound plan to be profitable by then, but likely sooner. I had not taken being vandalized into account.

I hopped out of the car so I could help Granny to the car. With friends, I would have simply sent a text that I was out front. That didn't work with Granny for so many reasons.

"Knock, knock." I said as I went inside.

"One minute, Mija!" Granny called from the back of the house.

Standing in the living room brought back so many happy memories. Dancing with my Aunt Rita, listening to my grandmother read, or Saturday movie nights with pizza in the living room. Coming home after school to Granny's warm cookies and doing my homework at the kitchen table. Sunday was always a large family dinner.

We called it family dinner, but there wasn't much family. A few distant cousins and sometimes my mother and Samuel would join us, even though this was my father's side of the family. She came for me. One of the few things she did for me.

My awful Uncle Sully and his wife, Gina sometimes joined us with their two awful children. My cousins technically, but I didn't feel a connection to them. They had always felt more like bullies that came to dinner.

We would also include friends that felt like family, which often meant Sawyer and Vee joined us. They loved Granny Ines's food, and they thought Aunt Rita was fun. But to be honest, they were here for many dinners, not just Sundays.

"Oh, Jessie, hi." Aunt Rita said, dancing into the room.

She was always swaying, bopping, or twirling around. I guess years of owning a dance studio had stuck with her. She had sold it a few years ago.

She took my hand, spinning me, and dancing me around the room. She hummed a familiar tune that I couldn't quite place. By the time the impromptu dance ended, I was laughing. Dancing with my Aunt Rita had been one of my favorite childhood memories.

"I haven't seen you in a while, since you're always so busy." she said, letting go of my hand, but she continued to sway.

"I know. I'm sorry. The restaurant takes a lot of my time."

"Did they figure out who broke in the other night?"

"Unfortunately, no. The two potential suspects had strong alibis and were backed up by credible witnesses." I sighed.

Detective Upton had called me this morning to let me know. He didn't give me many details about where they were, who backed up their stories, or anything. He simply said they had all provided evidence to show where they were.

"Oh, that must be frustrating."

"I can't even describe the frustration. I feel like someone is out to get me."

"But who? Who would hate you? You are such a loving and generous person." She patted my cheek gently.

I could think of a few people who thought otherwise, but I kept that to myself.

Noah was still concerned about Jenn. She'd already explained about the unknown vendor, and she hadn't given us any other reason to suspect her.

With no other names or ideas, all I could do at the moment was wait. The criminal was bound to slip up or the police department would find something.

"Thanks. It really is the million-dollar question."

"Oh, Jessie, is *that* what you are wearing to see your father?" Granny said, coming into the room.

I looked down at my outfit of a Neal Barney shirt with an image of bigfoot surrounded by black colored daisies and orange paisleys. It was paired with a long, black prairie skirt with black ankle boots.

"What's wrong with it?" I asked.

"I think she looks nice." Aunt Rita said.

"A t-shirt with a bear on it?"

"Wha …? It's not a bear." I looked down at my shirt. I loved this shirt. "It's bigfoot."

"It's fine. I'm sure your father will just be as happy to see you as I am." She came over to kiss my cheek. I had to lean down slightly, as she was several inches shorter than me.

"Are you ready to go?"

"Yes, let me get a bottle of water." She disappeared into the kitchen, returning a moment later with a bag with several bottles of water plus snacks. "Okay, do you need to go potty before we go?"

"Potty?" I chuckled. She still thought I was six years old.

"Oh, Mija, you know what I mean." She waved her hand dismissively.

"I'm good."

I hugged my aunt, then we were off. We were quiet for the first part of the trip. She stared out the window, watching the town go by. I loved this town, too. It was an artist's town which I loved. The buildings were cute, quaint, all brick, with arches and large windows.

We lived in a gorgeous brownstone on a block of nearly identical ones to ours. I loved our block. The tree-lined street and the window boxes with flowers.

Granny Ines and Aunt Rita lived in a small clapboard house on the edge of town. The houses there were single family with postage stamp yards. Many had white fencing around them. It was charming and sweet.

We drove across town, passing The Crock Pot. It looked decently busy for a Thursday afternoon. It was the early dinner crowd. I smiled as I continued on.

Once we were out of town, and the scenery changed to fields of crops and cows, she broke the silence.

"I heard you telling Margarita that they didn't find who broke into the restaurant." It was part question, part statement.

"Yes, the detective called me last night to let me know. He interviewed the suspects, and they had alibis, and those alibis were credible."

"That is so scary. What are you going to do?"

"Well, we have found another security monitoring company. They will be installing a new system tomorrow."

"That's good. I will feel better with you safe."

"I just want to cook and serve good food that makes people happy."

"That is what you have wanted to do for so long now." She reached over and patted my leg, smiling at me.

I nodded as I changed lanes.

Between my father's injury and the restaurant, it was too much. My life was once fairly simple. I cooked at a restaurant one town over, and I did cooking competitions several times a year. I liked to do them for the adrenaline rush and the prize money. Plus, it kept my skills sharp.

But now I had to worry about my employees, my business, and my father.

"Have you been able to talk to dad?"

"Only for a minute. He sounded okay," she said.

"Did he say anything about what happened?"

"No, they wouldn't let him. He is being watched closely now."

"Oh, does that mean he started it?"

"Maybe, but something I don't think you fully understand about your father. The reason he is in there is, he is about protecting others, taking on bullies, and defending people, which is probably what happened here, too."

I had heard something like this my whole life, but it didn't make sense to me. He killed a man. Took that man's life. Now his family was without their son, husband, and father. That didn't sound like a protector to me.

"Would you tell me what happened that night?" I didn't need to say which night. She knew.

"You've never asked before. Why now?"

"I guess I'm ready to have the gaps filled in. I can remember some of it, but I don't know why he did it. Only remembering what I said to the police and then to the judge." My mind brought the scene forward in my mind. I could see it so clearly, or so I thought. "We were hanging out with Mr. Jackson. Suddenly, they were fighting, then Mr. Jackson pulled out a gun. Dad got it and then … you know." I shrugged.

"Well, what you don't remember is that Mr. Jackson had you in his lap and was trying to *touch you*."

I gasped.

"Oh. Wow, I didn't know that. Well, I didn't remember. I guess I was too young to understand it." Tears stung my eyes.

"Yeah, so your father grabbed you and then started yelling at Mr. Jackson. You remember the rest."

I sat stunned for a moment, processing.

"I have been so mad at him, but all he was doing was defending me. I just didn't know." I couldn't think of anything else to say. All my life I had blocked that memory, but the memory came flooding back. "He told me it was okay. He told me he loved me. It wasn't the first time either. He had done it before. I just didn't know to stop him." I whispered.

She made a strangled gasping sound, as if fighting tears, then she reached for my free hand. We held hands, not speaking for a while.

How could I forget something so important? In that moment, I forgave my father for not being there for me. I thought he made this crazy, drunken mistake. Though I had no idea if he was drunk, that was how I justified it to myself all these years.

I looked at my grandmother briefly, thinking why hadn't I asked sooner. To be honest, even if she had explained it to me years ago, I wouldn't have been ready to listen. I would have thought she was lying.

Trauma is a strange thing. The holes in my memory were filling in now that I knew.

We sat quietly for several miles.

"Can we make a restroom break?" she asked at about the halfway point. It was only about a two to two- and half-hour drive away, but I was ready for a stretch, too.

I took the next exit and pulled into a gas station. We both got out. I grabbed a coffee for each of us while she visited the restroom.

Minutes later, we were back on the road and on to different topics, keeping things lighter as we drove the last hour of the drive. We pulled into the prison and checked in at the front desk. The process was mostly the same as it was to see him during normal visiting hours.

The difference was they had us go down a different hallway and wait in an area that looked much like any doctor's office. If not for the uniformed guards packing a firearm, you would have thought it was a hospital.

"Vasquez?" A nurse said at the door.

She led us into a room that had partitioned walls that didn't quite go to the ceiling. Everything was so white, making the glare of the fluorescent lights blinding. There was a guard stationed at a desk and another along the wall opposite my dad's hospital bed.

We turned to see him. I gasped. I had not expected him to be in such rough shape. His face was swollen, and they had his nose bandaged. Then he had an IV running to his arm with three bags of clear liquid. I couldn't tell what they contained, but I assumed maybe a pain med and perhaps an antibiotic. Not sure what the third could be.

"Oh, Mijo! Mi querido, my darling, are you okay?" Granny said, rushing to his side.

"Mamá, I am fine." His voice was a deep whisper. "My Jessie, you came to see your old man." He tried to chuckle, but it was flat.

"Yes, I was worried about you." I took his hand. He squeezed it. At least the officer allowed me to touch his hand.

I knew we couldn't get into details with the officer standing behind us, but just to see that he was okay was enough for me. We kept the topics shallow, safe things that were "approved" to discuss.

On television shows, I had seen that prisoners weren't as restricted, but this prison they had my father in had different rules. I didn't like it, but that's how it had been since he was locked up. Though when I was really young, they weren't as strict about touching.

He'd explained it when I was older that they didn't want a loved one to pass any contraband to the inmates. Less touching meant, less chance of that happening.

I wanted to ask him so many questions or tell him so many things, but I knew the officer would stop us. But as we started to wrap up, I decided to take my chance. What were they going to do, kick us out?

"Before we leave, thank you for defending me all those years ago." I looked over my shoulder. The officer looked like he might fall asleep.

"You remembered?" He asked.

I shook my head. "Granny told me on the way here."

"So, now you understand."

"I do. I love you."

"I love you, too. I would do it again for you."

"Is that what this was about?"

The officer cleared his throat. "That's time."

Ugh. I wanted to scream. We were making progress in our relationship for the first time in nearly thirty years.

I looked at my father and he simply nodded. At least I had my answer.

We quickly said our goodbyes and I promised him I would be back soon to visit.

"Will you and your friends come to Sunday dinner this week?" Granny asked once we were back on the road to Dashwood.

"I have to work the day shift, but can we do it after four?"

"I can if you come."

"We would love to."

"I will make those enchiladas that Sawyer loves with the cilantro rice that Vee likes." She giggled and clapped her hands together once.

"They will love it."

"Just like old times." She took my hand. "Wanna stop at Rosie's Diner when we get back to town?"

"I would love that. All the traditions." I laughed.

Chapter Twenty-Four

Noah and I watched the new security monitoring company install new cameras. They had already taken down the old ones and ran new wiring. We opted for this option because neither of us trusted that old system. We didn't even want a battery or lens left of it.

"This one will capture the back door, then I will put a second here, so it monitors the entire kitchen." The tech explained. He adjusted the camera, checking the video output on his tablet's screen. "See how it looks? What do you think?"

He held it so we could see it. Noah and I studied it together. We nodded at each other.

"Looks good."

"That's perfect."

"Great. I'll move over here." He climbed down from his ladder, moved it a few feet to the other camera, started adjusting it, checking on his tablet again, made a change, then checked it again. "Okay, how is that?"

Again, he held it for us to see. We looked. I looked over my shoulder around the room, then back to the screen.

"Can we see that one again? I just want to compare." I asked.

"Yes, of course." He clicked a few places, then held it out. "Side-by-side."

"Oh, nice." I looked at both outputs. "I think that works. Noah?"

"Um, actually, can you go a touch wider on this one? I feel like we are missing a view of the sink area."

"I am going to install one on that side which should capture it. However, if after I put that one in, you still want it changed, I can."

"Okay, I will wait then. Thanks."

I was excited by this new company. It was a national company that had high ratings and recommendations from the police department and Colt, Noah's friend.

We could still give individual codes, which I liked. Also, we weren't going to give Jenn any power to access it. That gave Noah some peace of mind. Though I felt it lost me some respect and trust with her.

"Is her trust more important than the business failing?" Noah had asked.

I knew he had a point, but I still hated to falsely accuse her of something. She'd not given me any reason to think she had anything to do with this.

The technician got down and began working on the next camera. We stood back, watching. After that was put in, I told Noah he could manage the rest while I started prepping.

I began with our soup of the day, chicken and wild rice. We also did the alphabet soup daily. It was my favorite and my award-winning recipe, so I had to do it.

I started chopping all the vegetables first. I had won a few awards for my speed chopping back in high school. My knife flew through the onions and sliced up the celery. It calmed me.

Parker came in as I was halfway through. He jumped right into making the soup. I moved on to starting side dishes. Then Hannah, another line cook, came in, and helped me with those.

Our entire prepping process had been streamlined. We could now get everything ready for the day in just over an hour. Hannah was in charge of keeping us stocked all day with food. Parker and I focused on the cooking. We also had another junior line cook who made salads and cold sandwiches.

The day flew by after that with dish after wonderful dish, and it was now time for the evening shift. June and I did our normal turnover.

"Today was busy. Hannah had to make more soup twice."

"Nice. I hope we are that busy tonight! It makes the time go by and keeps me young." She shimmied her whole body as she laughed.

I chuckled with her. She had such a fun energy. I miss Earl daily, but I'm glad we found her.

"Yes, time definitely flies by." I hugged her. "I'm so glad you're here. You have been an awesome addition."

Stelly leaned over. "I agree. You are such a joy to work with, and I'm learning a lot."

"Y'all are so sweet. I love working here."

"Well, I'm going to touch base with Noah and then head home. Night, ladies." I waved as I headed towards the sink to wash my hands then to the office.

Noah was giving Jenn the information about the new camera. She had limited access to it this time, but we had tried to spin it positively. She was smiling, but she was keeping still and appeared tense.

"The employee codes are all the same, but only Jess and mine will control the system." He said.

"Okay." she mumbled.

"Do you have any questions?" He asked.

She stared at him. Her lips quivered as she started to speak.

"I'm sorry for whatever I did to make you both distrust me. I don't know what it was, but I'm just sorry." She hung her head as tears fell.

My heart ached. I closed the gap, wrapping my arms around her. My action startled both her and me as I wasn't the hugging type.

"It wasn't anything you did. We are just trying to be careful. We don't know who is doing things to the business, to me, but the fewer people with full access, the better."

She sniffled a bit. "Okay. I guess that makes sense, but I just … I don't want you to think I did anything."

"No, and hopefully this will be over soon, and we can all get back to normal." I let her go and smiled at her. "You good now?"

"Yeah, I'm good." She smiled, but her flat tone had me concerned.

I knew this was a bad idea. It really hurt the trust that I had tried to build with all the employees, but especially the two managers. However, I had to trust someone and at this point it was Noah.

Of course, why was I so quick to trust him? He was the only one asking for changes and shining doubt on the other manager.

It was a tough position to be in.

"Okay, well, I'm going to head out. Call me if you have any troubles or questions." Noah said, as he gathered his stuff.

I grabbed my purse and said my goodbyes as well. We walked out together. He looked over his shoulder as we reached our cars.

"She's a good actress." He murmured.

"You think she was acting?"

"You don't?"

Maybe I was naïve, but I believed her. He had yet to show me proof that she was involved. All he had done was speculate. I had chosen to trust him, but that didn't mean I didn't think she was innocent also.

"I really don't. I believe it is Flora and possibly Eric. Now that he is gone, things should get back to normal around here, especially since we have a better security system."

"I hope you're right." He shrugged, then climbed into his car. I watched him go, looked once at the restaurant before I drove away, too.

As I pulled out onto the street, my phone rang. I didn't recognize the number and hesitated to answer it, but what if it was something business related?

"Hello?"

"We will not be stopped by a new system." A computer-generated voice said.

My blood ran cold.

"Who is this? Who won't be stopped?"

"It is not time to reveal ourselves yet, but in time. Now stop trying to get in our way. We will not be deterred."

"What did I do to you? Why are you so angry at me?" A lump formed in my throat.

"You know what you did."

The line went dead.

My body started shaking.

What the bleep?

What do I do now? I kept driving home and tried not to think about it. My phone rang again. The display said Sawyer.

"Hello?"

"Hey, Jessie, are you off?"

"I am." My voice cracked.

"Whoa, are you okay?"

"I just got a weird phone call."

"Weird, how?"

"A computer voice just threatened me, or at least I felt threatened." Now I couldn't remember if they actually said anything except, they wouldn't be deterred. Nothing about harming me physically. Still isn't that threatening?

"Did you call that detective guy?"

"No, I didn't think about it. I mean, what can they do?"

He sighed. "You're probably right. They can't do much, but at least there would be a report of it."

"Maybe, but that's not why you called. What's up?"

"Oh, yeah, do you want to go out to eat tonight? Take a break. Treat ourselves."

"That would be nice. Yes." I sighed.

We hung up as I pulled to the curb in front of our townhouse. I headed into shower and to get ready for dinner out with my friends.

Vee came into the bathroom while I was dressing. She gossiped about this or that. Mostly things at work. I listened but didn't have much to say or add to the conversation. She didn't care; she loved to talk. It was one of my favorite things about her.

Once I was dressed, Sawyer came in to join us.

"Did she tell you about the phone call she got today?" Sawyer said to Vee.

"No, was it juicy?" She giggled.

Sawyer and I frowned at each other.

"Oh, no, was it bad news? It wasn't your father again, was it?" she asked.

"No, just a computer voice telling me I can't stop them, and they will not be … what word did they use?" I thought. "Oh, yes, deterred. That was it."

"Yikes. Who keeps doing this to you?" Vee asked.

"I wish I knew. According to the detective, Flora and Eric both have strong alibis for Monday night, so I feel like we are back at square one."

"Plus, Flora took credit for the spray paint." Sawyer pointed out.

"Yeah, and I feel like if it was her, she is the type that would want the credit." I exhaled.

"What about that Reggie guy?" Vee asked.

"I'm not sure. The detective hadn't mentioned talking to him." To be honest, I couldn't remember if I even mentioned him to Upton.

"You should ask him."

"Yeah, I should." I sighed again. I really didn't want to think about this any longer. I was off work, and I wanted to relax. "But on to other business, where are we going?"

"What about Beaks and Brews?" Vee asked.

"Sounds good to me."

"Yeah, me too."

I tried to enjoy my evening with my friends, but my mind kept replaying the conversation. The voice was going to haunt my nightmares.

At least the chicken was fried to perfection, and the in-house brewed beer really hit the spot. Chef Nathan came out to greet me and congratulate me on my restaurant.

"I have been out there. Good stuff. That soup." He did the chef's kiss action.

"Aw, thanks. Let me know the next time you come out, I'll come say hi."

"I will." He gave a salute and headed back into the kitchen.

After dinner, we ended up at Pins for some bowling and another beer or two. There were a lot of laughs and a lot of bad bowling. Vee won with the highest score.

It was a good evening overall.

Chapter Twenty-Five

"Hurry up, Vee. We're going to be late." Sawyer yelled up the stairs. "I can't miss out on Ines's enchiladas."

"She will have plenty." I laughed. "Don't worry."

"They are so good. I have been thinking about them for days."

Vee finally came down the stairs.

"Sorry, sorry. I'm ready."

"You had all day while I was at work. Why didn't you get ready before I got home?"

"I don't know. Bad planning."

I couldn't argue with that. She was never one to be ready on time.

We hopped in the car and Sawyer put the car in gear.

"Hey, turn this up!" Vee yelled as she began to sing along with the song.

"High school vibes!" I yelled, joining her in singing.

Sawyer laughed at our offbeat, off-key version. We messed up a few lyrics, but we were laughing together, and that was the best. I had been so stressed for weeks. It was nice to let my hair down.

Sawyer signaled to take a right onto Willis Street. When we turned, a car passed us, aggressively whipping in front of us, then slamming on their brakes. Sawyer was fast enough to respond so as not to hit them.

"What in the bleep?" I said.

The car pulled forward quickly, then slamming on their brakes again.

"Should we call 9-1-1?" Vee asked.

"I don't know," he said.

"Did you cut them off or something?" I asked.

"Not that I know of. They came out of nowhere."

This continued a third time, before Sawyer turned onto a different street and then doubled back.

"Okay, maybe we lost them now?" He looked around.

As we came back onto Broadway, the car came up on our left side, swerving at us.

"What the heck?" Sawyer cursed. He drove down another street with the car following closely. "I'm just going to drive to the police station. You should call 9-1-1, maybe?"

"Got it." Vee said from the back seat.

I could hear her side of the conversation as she told them that someone was harassing us.

"Yes, we are on Broadway, heading south to the police station. They are swerving at us." Vee squealed as the car came inches from us again. "Okay. We will."

She hung up. "They said just keep going to the police station. They will have officers outside to meet us."

"Got it." he said, as he steered the car down the street.

He maneuvered the car expertly through the streets. We were able to get into some traffic, though traffic was a strong word for what we had in Dashwood. Having spent time in big cities like New York, Houston, and Los Angeles, this was nothing, but it kept us from getting hit. Sawyer managed to keep a few cars between us.

The police station came into view, and we could see a few officers standing around in the parking lot. They were looking up and down the street. The car had managed to catch up to us, just before we reached the parking lot. They clipped our back bumper which sent us into a slow spin.

Vee and I squealed from inside the car as we spun around.

I couldn't see what was happening, but I heard the squeal of tires as we came to a stop hitting a pole. It wasn't hard as Sawyer managed things well.

Have I mentioned what an excellent driver he is?

"Is everyone okay?" Sawyer asked breathlessly.

"I think I am." Though I might have hit my head on the window. I kept that to myself for now.

I rubbed the spot as I looked around. Officers were running towards us, and a police car took off, heading in the direction the car drove off in.

"I hit my head a little, but I'm okay." Vee said.

"Oh, I hit mine, too." I confessed.

"You said you were okay." Sawyer said.

"I know, but since she hit hers, I thought I would share."

We climbed out of the car as the officers arrived. Sawyer assessed the damage with one of the officers that I hadn't met before, while Officer Lupe Perez came to talk to Vee and me.

"Are you both okay?" she asked.

"We both hit our heads, but I think we are okay." Vee spoke for us, as I was in a bit of shock.

"Did you see who was driving?"

"No, the car had dark windows, but it looked like there may have been two people?" She looked at me.

I nodded. Perez noted that in her notepad.

"Can you describe the car?"

"A dark, two-door sedan. I couldn't tell the model because they didn't have the little emblems on it. It had paper tags that I couldn't read. I did get a picture." She pulled out her phone, showing Officer Perez. Together they scrolled through the pictures.

"It looked a lot like the one I've seen before. The one that shot at Vivian and me."

"This is helpful." Officer Perez nodded.

My phone rang. It was Granny Ines.

"It's my grandmother. We're supposed to be at her house right now. May I take this?"

Officer Perez nodded, so I walked a few feet away to take the call.

"Hi, Granny."

"Jessie, where are you?"

"I'm sorry, we had a minor car accident."

"Are you okay?"

"Yes, yes. Just giving statements to the police and then we'll be on our way. The car just got bumped, and we are fine."

"Okay, well, everyone is here, and we will be praying you arrive soon and safe."

We ended our call, and I walked back to the group.

"Okay, we have your statements, her pictures, and a description of the car. We will get working on this."

"What about the officers that went after them? Were they able to catch up?" Sawyer asked.

"No, they lost them." Perez confirmed. I frowned. "But they are still out looking. We will let you know if we find them."

I nodded.

"So, we are free to go then?" Vee asked.

"Yes, we are done and will be in touch if we find anything out."

We were all just thankful the car was still drivable and there was only some minor damage. That could have been a lot worse.

We got into the car and headed to my grandmother's house. Most of the drive over, we were quiet. I guess like me, they were both processing what happened.

As we turned on my grandmother's street, I could see several cars in her driveway.

"Oh, Uncle Sully is here." I said. "I didn't know they were coming."

"Do you think *everyone* is here?" Vee asked.

"Probably."

That meant my cousins were here. Nova and Sullivan Junior were not my favorite people. They had always been jealous that I got to live with Granny Ines and teased me for my deadbeat father. Those were likely my Aunt Gina's words being repeated by them.

"They are the worst." Sawyer moaned as he steered the car to the curb.

We all looked up at the house. Even the promise of enchiladas wasn't enough to offset the annoyance of my cousins. We let out a collective sigh and shared a brave smile with each other as we climbed out.

"Knock, knock." I said as I pushed open the door.

"There you are." Granny Ines came forward to hug us, then studied us. "Are you all okay?"

"Yeah, Vee and I hit our heads a bit, but not bad. It was a minor thing. Nothing serious."

I didn't need her worrying about this and I didn't even know what had happened. All I could hope was that the police could find whoever it was. Until then, I would keep that to myself.

She stood on her tiptoes to kiss my forehead. "Well, you all come in here. We are nearly ready to eat."

We followed her to the dining room where my Uncle Sully, Aunt Gina, and my two awful cousins, Nova and Junior, were sitting. My Aunt Rita waltzed in with a tray of drinks. She saw us and giggled.

"Oh, I'm so happy to see y'all." She set the drinks down and swayed her way to us, hugging us each in turn. "Here sit, sit."

"Hello, Uncle Sully and Aunt Rita." I nodded to them, only smiling at my cousins.

"Jessie, how are you?" Uncle Sully asked.

"I'm good. It's been a while since I've seen you all."

"Well, you could come around more often." Aunt Gina snipped.

"Yes, well, I'm busy with my restaurant."

"Death-aurant." Nova giggled.

"What?"

"You heard me." She snapped.

"That's enough, Nova. Jessie has done wonderful things, and one death is not her fault." Aunt Rita said, setting down a platter of enchiladas.

I smiled at her. She winked and went back into the kitchen to help Granny bring in the rest of the food.

She had always stuck up for me and been my biggest fan.

"Here we go. Tacos, tamales, and enchiladas with rice and beans." Granny Ines said, setting down a platter of food and pointing to each item. "Let us pray."

Everyone bowed their heads, but I took one look around before closing my eyes. Junior was looking right at me and stuck out his tongue. I was too shocked to react as he closed his eyes and bowed his head. Granny spoke of family blessings and of the love at this table, and all I wanted to do was cry.

Except for her, my father, and Aunt Rita, I didn't always feel love from my family. My friends were more like my family than my own blood. Just look at how Nova and Junior treated me in less than two minutes.

I had too much on my mind with the restaurant and being harassed by who knows who and if not Flora or Eric, I had no idea who else would bother me.

I mean maybe that Reggie guy, but honestly, I had only met him once. Why and what did he have to gain from it? Nothing.

Could it be my own family? I peeked at them quickly before everyone opened their eyes. Thankfully, Junior kept his tongue in his mouth.

No, I know that I was treated like the family scapegoat at times, but I couldn't see them wasting time stalking me. They just openly did it. Well, only when Granny wasn't looking.

The prayer ended with a round of amens, then the food started to get passed around. Talking was limited to please, pass and thank you as everyone started eating.

After the first serving, that's when talking started.

"Granny Ines, this is amazing. Thank you for having us." Sawyer said with a smile.

"Aw, thank you. I love having you kids here. I just wish we could see you more."

"With June working out so well, I might be able to come more often now." I smiled.

"I would love that." Granny clapped her hands together.

"We both would." Aunt Rita touched my arm. "We love seeing you."

My cousins smirked at each other but didn't say a word.

"Sully, have you gone to see your brother?" Granny asked him.

"No, mother, why should I?" Sully huffed. "He is dead to me."

Everyone stopped and looked at him. There was about to be a fight. I looked over at Vee and Sawyer. They had been here for other fights, so it wasn't new to them.

"Sullivan Leonard Vasquez, that is your brother. He is family and you don't turn your back on family!"

"He took a life. That is no family of mine." Sully pointed his finger at her.

"Don't you point your finger at me!" She hissed. Her accent strong as her anger flared. "He is my son and your brother. He was protecting Jessie. That is honorable."

"Always with Jessie. Jessie, this. Jessie, that. If something was happening, he should have let the police manage it."

My mouth fell open at his words. What had I done? I was only 5 years old at the time. He was saying this like I caused the problems.

"Why are you blaming Jessie? She was just a tiny child then. You need to forgive!" Granny slammed her hand on the table.

"Mother, you are always on his side. Where were you when I needed you? When my children needed you?"

"They had you and Gina. What do they need me for?"

"To be a grandmother to them. You catered to Jess and her friends, leaving little time for my children."

"Wait a minute, Sully, I was here too. Mother had plenty of time for your children. You didn't allow them here." Rita stepped in.

"You shouldn't even have a say in this at all. You didn't marry, you don't have children. You have just been mom's lackey for life!"

There was a collective gasp around the table. Granny pushed up, storming off. Rita began crying. The cousins were giggling. Aunt Gina started nagging her husband while he tried to backtrack his words. It was too late. Granny was off stewing and Auntie Rita had tears streaming down her face as she pouted from her seat.

I was too shocked to speak. Sawyer helped himself to more enchiladas and Vee just looked at me. As I was processing the scene, my phone rang. It was Detective Upton.

I excused myself, though only my friends heard me.

"Hello, Detective." I answered.

"Hi, Jess. So, a little news on the car. We found it, but unfortunately, it was on fire. Any evidence has been burned in the fire. Though once it cools, we are hoping to get VIN numbers from it. Maybe we can find out who it is registered to."

"What? Seriously?"

"Yes. We tracked it on some of the cameras around town, but then it left town. That's how we traced it. Then a report came of a car on fire."

I said a silent curse. Just my luck. I wanted this over.

"We will keep looking for the people responsible, but at this point, it is a dead end."

"Any more news on Earl's killer or my security cameras? Anything?"

"I'm sorry. No, nothing yet."

I counted to ten and gulped down a curse. Well, I didn't actually curse, but a lot of bleeps were said in my head.

"Okay, well, thanks, detective."

We ended the call. I turned to see Aunt Rita standing behind me, tears in her eyes. She came over and hugged me. No dancing, no swaying. She was hurt.

"I'm sorry he said those things. You are amazing." I said, hugging her.

"You know Granny and I both love you."

"Yes, of course. He is just a mean, unhappy man. Wouldn't you be if those were your children." I whispered, not wanting anyone to hear me say it, even if I meant it.

I had been taught to respect those older than me. He obviously hadn't learned that lesson.

She giggled at my words.

"You okay?" I asked.

"Yeah, yes, or I will be. It isn't like he hasn't said all those things before. It just always hurts when he says it." She tried to smile. "You know, I wanted a family of my own. It just never happened for me."

"I know. And you were a wonderful part of my life. I'm so thankful for you."

She smiled.

My uncle and his family left after that. Junior stuck his tongue out at me as they were leaving. Sawyer caught him doing it.

"What are you, twelve?" he laughed.

"No, you know how old I am."

"Well, act like it."

Junior huffed and followed his family out.

We stayed to help cleanup and then when Granny came out of her room, we played a few hands of poker. It turned into a fun night. We didn't speak about the family fight or the accident or even what the detective shared with me.

On the drive home, we looked all around us. Paranoid was going to be our way of life until they caught this person or people doing this.

Chapter Twenty-Six

When we got home from Granny's, I received a text from Noah. Colt had found something on the security camera footage.

N: **It isn't extremely clear, but it's something**

Me: **Wanna meet early tomorrow at the restaurant?**

N: **Yep. See ya at 8?**

Me: **Sounds good**

With that thought, I fell asleep.

I was deep asleep when something woke me. My brain was foggy as I stumbled around my room trying to find the source. Then I realized it was my phone. Grabbing it from where it fell on the floor, it showed that the security alarm was going off at the restaurant.

"Son of a bleepity-bleep." I mumbled. Then the phone rang, showing the alarm company's number.

I gave them the security pass code.

"We have a motion alert on cameras two and five. Would you like us to send the police?"

I was pulling on clothes as I listened.

"Yeah, I'm going to head over there now, but it is probably nothing."

"Does that mean you don't want us to send the police?"

"Sorry, yes, please send them. I'm going too. I can meet them there."

"Great. I will let the dispatch know you will meet them."

I grabbed my car keys and purse, then jogged down the stairs.

"Oh, you're still awake." I said when I found Sawyer on the couch.

"Yeah, epic game going right now. Silas and I are taking on a couple of players in Germany." He rapidly pushed the buttons. "Take that. Yay!"

"Well, I have to run over to the restaurant. Security alarm going off."

"Dang, I thought you got that fixed."

"Yeah, I did too. The company is sending the police to meet me."

"Want me to drive you?"

"Um, no, you and Silas beat the other team. Save the world from electronic zombies." I pumped my fist in the air as a show of support. Then I started out the door.

"Will do. Call if you need me." He rapidly pushed the buttons. "Take that!"

I chuckled as I jogged down the steps to my car. Roughly five or so minutes later, I pulled into the parking lot. There were no cars in the lot, but there was one across the street next to the eye doctor.

I stared at it, trying to see if anyone was in it or anywhere nearby. After a moment or two, a car came from up the street, passing, but never slowed or looked my way.

I stayed in my car waiting for the police to show up, but when the alarm went off again and I didn't see any movement, I figured it was malfunctioning.

Darn my luck.

The security alarm company called.

"We have called the police dispatch again. They said officers are on their way."

"Okay. I'm going to head inside. It's maybe some dust or something."

The police station wasn't that far away, but I didn't hear any sirens. I hesitated at the back door, trying to wait for them, but a noise inside caught my attention.

I don't know what possessed me to open the door, but I opened it. There was light coming from the office and maybe the dining room.

Clutching my cell phone with my finger hovering over the emergency call button, I stepped inside.

"Hello?" I called out. Again, probably stupid, but I wasn't thinking.

"Well, well, well, we meet again." Reggie stood in front of me. I recognized him right away.

"Damn it!" A familiar voice said from somewhere in the darkness.

I squinted my eyes, trying to see who else was here.

"We weren't expecting you to show up." Flora stepped forward, but she wasn't the voice I had heard. How many people were here?

"The alarm was going off." I said.

"I knew you hadn't turned it off." Flora yelled out.

"That isn't my fault. They changed all the passwords and the company." That's when I realized who the voice belonged to. It was Jenn.

I said a silent curse.

Someone grabbed me from behind, pushing me to my knees. In the process, my phone fell to the floor.

Bleep! I hope it didn't break. I couldn't ask them or look at it myself. Then I cursed myself for even worrying about it when I had bigger problems than a busted phone.

"Tie her up so we can finish." Reggie said.

"We would already be finished if you two weren't idiots." Jenn yelled from the office.

"If the alarm went off, that means the cops are probably on their way. We need to get out of here. I can't afford another run in." A male voice said behind me.

"Eric?"

"Ha, surprise, Chef." He laughed in a way that sent a chill down my spine. "But my name isn't Eric. It's Alistair Jackson."

"Jackson? As in —?"

"Yeah, as in my brother and the son of the man your father murdered!" Flora taunted.

"Yeah, we lost our father because of you!" Eric, or I guess, Alistair said.

"It wasn't my fault. I was only a child myself."

"Well, I wasn't born and never got to know my father." Flora said.

I bite my tongue to stop myself from telling them about the crimes against their father. Though my memories had come back completely, I had no proof. Plus, he wasn't alive to face charges anyway.

She should be thanking me and my father. I likely saved her from also being abused in the same way. Okay, I really didn't think my father should have taken care of Mr. Jackson that way. He should have let him stand trial instead.

But I had bigger problems at the moment as I was being held at gunpoint.

"I knew him. He was the best." Alistair said.

"I lost my father, too."

"No, you didn't. He's just in prison, and you can see him almost anytime you want," Flora snapped.

"Even though we tried to take care of that, it backfired on us," Reggie added.

"Y'all had my father attacked?"

"We tried, but the bastard is tough. Hurt our guy pretty badly."

"Good." I said, which won me a backhand across the face by Alistair.

"Don't think I won't kill you, just like I did Earl," Alistair said stepping back.

"You killed Earl?"

"Yes, I did. He overheard a conversation that he shouldn't have."

"Yeah, wrong place, wrong time earned him a bullet in the head." Flora laughed.

"You killed him over a conversation?"

"Well, it was a little more than just a conversation. We were passing some cash and plotting." Alistair laughed.

"I don't understand."

"We were stealing from you. Duh." Reggie said. "He overheard and tried to intervene. That's actually a more accurate account of how he got himself killed."

"Y'all are sick. Just like your father."

This time, it was Flora who hit me, and more than once. She jumped on me pushing me to the ground as she continued the assault.

Alistair had to pull her off of me. I couldn't fight back with my hands tied behind my back. Tears burned my eyes at the frustration of this situation. I could kick her butt if I wasn't tied up.

She wiped her own tears as she stood above me.

"You don't know what my life was like! Until you spend every birthday and each and every holiday celebrating at a cemetery while your mother cries, you don't know anything about me. Call me sick if you want, but that was my life!" She growled.

"Well, I am sorry you had to go through that. I spent most of my birthdays and holidays at the prison, and my mother tossed me aside. Life sucks like that sometimes, but I didn't kill or steal anything because of it."

"Well, you turned to food." She eyed me up and down. "Some of us took *another* path."

"Babe, bring her in here. I am struggling with this safe." Jenn yelled from the office.

"Babe?"

"Um, yeah, my girlfriend." Alistair laughed. I was still struggling to remember his name wasn't Eric. "Is that okay with you, *Chef*?"

"I just didn't know how you all knew each other."

"Well, Alistair and I are brother and sister. Reggie is my boyfriend. Jenn is Alistair's girlfriend. Oh, and Reggie and Alistair were friends for years." Flora filled me in.

"Why are y'all telling her everything?" Reggie asked.

"I don't know. I mean, it won't matter much longer anyway." Flora made the shape of a gun with her hand, aiming it at me as she snickered.

Alistair and Reggie both grabbed me roughly, pulling me to my feet and pushing me forward. As we moved through the kitchen, I could see they had trashed it again.

"Damn it, could you stop trashing my kitchen?"

"Ha, we can't do that. We want to ruin you." Reggie hissed in my ear.

"Ruin me? By stealing from me?"

"Not just stealing, but messing up your business, trying to break you, and tarnish the great Chef Jessica reputation." Alistair chuckled in my other ear.

"You should have just hired me. It would have been easier." Flora laughed.

"What, so you could *all* have easy access to my business? This is bad enough. I should have listened to Noah."

"Yeah, he is much smarter than you." Jenn laughed as we came into the office. "And he'll be next."

The whole place was trashed. The filing cabinets had been emptied. Everything on or in the desks was now on the floor and they were trying to get into the safe.

I'm glad I listened to him on changing the safe pass code. It meant she no longer knew it, which was making this harder for her. If she missed it enough times, it wouldn't open without a special code and would set off another alarm.

"What is the code?" She snapped, pointing at the safe. "And I know what happens if you do it wrong."

"Is that why the office is a mess? You were looking for the code?"

She manically laughed. "Maybe you are smarter than I thought. Now open it."

My mind went blank and all I could think was, where the heck were the police? Shouldn't they be here by now?

"Oh, um, how am I going to open it with my hands tied behind my back?"

"Ugh. Never mind you aren't smart, are you? Unless this is a stalling technique. You just tell me the code."

I looked over my shoulder at the others standing nearby. I wasn't getting out of this alive no matter what I did, but I felt if I complied, I had a better shot.

"Six, five, six, seven, nine, one."

She eyed me for a second, trying to decide if she believed me. After a heartbeat, she punched it in and the safe unlocked.

"Ta-da!"

"Bingo!"

"Oh, yay!"

"We did it."

They got busy grabbing stuff out of the safe, except Reggie who pulled out a gun.

"I'm going to enjoy this!" He chuckled as he stood above me.

I closed my eyes, but before I heard anything more, there was a loud bang around us. Not like a gunshot, but something else. I opened my eyes to see the room was filling with smoke or gas.

"Hands up. Hands up!" Someone yelled at the door.

Suddenly the room was filled with officers. Someone pulled me out of the room, and I could hear yelling and commotion from inside the office.

"Are you okay, Chef?" a voice asked.

My eyes were watering from the smoke so I couldn't quite see who it was, and my ears were still ringing from the bangs.

"I think so. I can't see."

"I'll help you outside. It will clear in the air."

"Detective Upton?"

"Yes, it's me. I'll help you outside."

He guided me out the door. My eyes kept watering and burning.

"Don't fight it. Let them water. It will help." He said. "Sorry, we had to do that with you in there. We didn't have a choice."

I heard him call for a water bottle. He helped me wash my eyes with the water. He then handed me a paper towel. I wiped my face.

"Thanks. I thought I was a goner for sure."

"Thankfully, your phone called us."

"But the alarm company had called too, right?"

"Yeah, I guess the dispatch was slow in putting out the call, but we got a call from your phone and heard some of what was happening. They called me immediately."

"I didn't realize I had hit the button. I dropped my phone when they grabbed me."

"Well, we have them now and the dispatchers have a recording of what was said. We now know who killed your friend and we know who has been terrorizing you."

At that moment, officers came out the back door with the four in handcuffs. Flora started cursing and yelling things in my direction. Detective Upton moved me further away from them.

Thanks to the water, my eyes had cleared enough to see them as they were loaded into the police cruisers and driven away. Justice was served, or at least the start of justice.

I gave a statement, then they allowed me inside to lock up my cash and put things back into the safe. The officers started processing the scene.

I watched helplessly from a corner of the kitchen. When the clock showed a reasonable time to do so, I sent a text to Noah. He replied he was on his way over.

Within fifteen minutes, Noah was here, hugging me.

"Are you okay?"

"Yeah, I'm okay."

"I knew it was Jenn. I just knew it."

"You were right. I should have listened."

"I'll give them the footage that Colt found." Noah said.

"Yeah, I guess we don't need to review it now."

"Nope. When I saw it, I thought one of the figures might have been Eric, but I couldn't quite tell."

"Alistair."

"What?"

"His name is Alistair Jackson. He is Flora's brother and the son of the man my father killed."

"Holy … wow!" He ran his hand down his face. "I guess that makes sense. Jenn doesn't seem to fit in with the others. Any idea?"

"Yeah, she is dating Alistair, or Eric, as we know him. Alistair is friends with Reggie who is Flora's boyfriend."

"So, they just had a grudge or what?"

"Yeah, basically. Jenn has been stealing from us too. All those weird accounting entries you saw, that is part of it."

"I knew it!" He cheered. "Oh, sorry, Chef. I shouldn't be excited about that."

"No, you should. I'm just sorry I didn't listen. I won't make that mistake again."

Hours later, the police were done, and we had let the entire staff know we would be closed for two days. We needed time to clean and assess the damage.

I didn't expect our vendor would be able to replace the food as quickly this time, even if I offered top dollar, which I couldn't afford.

I was just glad that this was over, and we could put this behind us. At least, that was my hope. I was so gun-shy about all of this.

Would someone else come out of the woodwork now? I sure hope not. Four people was enough, right?

Chapter Twenty-Seven

It has been a week since Flora, Jenn, Alistair/Eric, and Reggie were arrested. It was such a relief to have that behind me. I could finally sleep peacefully.

My father had recovered and moved back to his normal life in prison, but I had a different view of him now. He was my hero in so many ways, despite his crime.

Could he have handled it differently? Oh yeah, I wouldn't have asked him to do what he did, but in his mind, it was the only choice. I could forgive him for his thinking.

Everyone is a hero in their own story.

The restaurant was reopened, and we were busier than ever. It was like the town had rallied around us in a show of support for what we had been through. But also, everyone wanted a bit of gossip, an inside scoop. There wasn't anything new to share, but they all hoped.

Nadine from *Dining with Nadine* and Lynette from *What's on the Table in Dashwood,* both came out for another interview and review of The Crock Pot. It was, in part, what sparked the increase in business.

"This is my favorite meal I have ever had," Lynette said. "The soup is superb, and the half sandwich pairs perfectly with it."

"We are so glad you enjoyed it." I smiled.

"I'm so glad they caught those crooks. I can't believe all they put you through."

"Thanks. Your support means so much."

I didn't want to mention how stressful it was or how many times I wished I could give up. Being the boss was harder than I could ever imagine it would be.

Had I just been an employee, these past few months would have been annoying, but I could just do my job and someone else would be responsible.

Instead, I had to deal with the police, with the mess, with the loss of business and inventory. I spent countless hours worried about my staff members and whether they were safe. It was a nightmare.

I never thought I would have to investigate a murder or find vandals. I fumbled my way through it, and while I didn't exactly figure it out, I think I was getting close. That's likely why they thought it was time for that big break-in, before they missed their chance.

If only I had gotten out of my naïve mindset about Jenn. Noah was not going to let me forget this.

Thank goodness I won't have to do that again. I thought. One murder case was enough.

Today we were interviewing employees for most positions. With the increase in business, we needed it. We decided to add two more servers on the day shift and one for the night shift. Then an additional busser and line cook for each shift.

I had also officially promoted Parker to sous chef. He would fill in for June or me when needed. It meant the two of us could now take off full days, instead of just half days and the odd full day when needed.

It was a huge relief to have him ready for this responsibility, and with the foursome in jail, it made it easier to promote him.

My phone chimed. It was Colt, Noah's cybersecurity friend.

C: **We still on for Sunday?**

Me: **Yep, looking forward to finally meeting you.**

C: **Me too**

Yes, I was going on a date for the first time in forever. It was more of a favor to Noah and as a thank you to Colt for his help with the security camera footage. However, after a few texts back and forth with Colt, we kind of clicked and now I got a slight flutter in my stomach when I saw his name pop up.

It was a strange feeling as I hadn't dated in a few years, and even before that, I hadn't had a serious relationship in nearly eight years.

He followed the reply with a silly gif of a dancing hamster. I quietly laughed.

"What's that smile for?" Noah said, as he sat next to me in the dining room.

"Nothing."

"Um, yeah, I believe you." He chuckled, nudging me with his elbow.

"You ready for this next interview?"

"Yeah, but I'll be glad when we get to the assistant manager interviews next week. I need help."

"With Parker's promotion, I thought I was helping you." I was almost offended.

"You are, but a full-time assistant manager would help us both so much."

I couldn't argue with that, and I wasn't even going to try. The first interviewee of the day came in and we began. It was good to get back into a routine and feel like things were going to be okay,

THE END

Before you go: If you loved Appetizers and Alibis, be sure to visit my website to sign up for my newsletter and to stay up to date on new releases and other bookish things. When signing up, you will receive **Chef Jessica's Alphabet Soup Recipe** as a free gift. I have "had" it; it is yummy. (Okay, so obviously, it is my recipe, but still, I recommend it!)

Continue to the next section for this book's recipe!

www.ejwheltonwrites.com

Recipe:

I make this a few times a year. It is so good. I use different types of cheddar cheese, mixing white cheddar, sharp cheddar, and/or extra sharp. You can do the same, but you need it to equal about 2 cups. You can also tweak some of the spices to your taste.

Enjoy! If you make it email me at ejwheltonwrites@gmail.com and let me know what you think.

Pimento Cheese:

8 oz cream cheese, softened
2 cups of sharp cheddar cheese (do not use the prepackaged cheese. It is best if you freshly grate it.)
2 oz jar of pimento peppers, drained
3 tablespoons mayonnaise
1 tablespoon sour cream
½ teaspoon salt
¼ teaspoon onion powder
½ teaspoon garlic powder
Hot sauce (like Frank's Red hot or Louisiana Hot Sauce), to taste. I usually do about a tablespoon, but taste if I need more.

Instructions:
1. Beat softened cream cheese. (I use a hand mixer, but you can use a stand mixer)
2. Add the other ingredients. I stir as I add each one.
3. Once combined well, cover and chill in fridge for at least a few hours. Overnight is best.
4. Serve with crackers, toasted slices of bread, or with sliced sweet peppers (my favorite).

Author note:

This one was fun to write! I hope you enjoyed reading it as much as I enjoyed writing it. If you haven't heard the inspiration behind it, I was watching Beat Bobby Flay and one of the chefs was a Chef Jessica. Now, my Jessica is not that one, but something about the name sent me into a note writing frenzy as my Chef Jess came to life almost before my eyes. It was magical.

Sawyer and Vee then introduced themselves, and I drew inspiration from my kitty cat, June for Lulu. The rest, as they say, is history.

I want to thank my parents, my husband, my children, and my dear, dear friends for all their support once again with this one.

And a special shout out to Mariah Sinclair for the gorgeous cover! She took my vision and brought it to life.

This is going to be a long series, and I am excited to see Jessica hone her sleuthing skills with each story and murder. She fumbled a bit as she tried to find her feet in this one, but Biscuits and Bodies is next, and it is shaping up to be another fun adventure.

Thank you for reading and for your amazing support.

www.ejwheltonwrites.com